Sacred
HEARTS

Sacred Hearts

TARNISHED SOULS

Dev Bentham

www.devbentham.com

Sacred Hearts

Copyright © December 2012 by Dev Bentham

Rereleased as ISBN 978-1-942255-02-4
Cover Artist: Jordan Castillo Price
Printed in the United States of America

Published by
Love is a Light Press
POB 685
Minocqua, WI
www.devbentham.com

This is a work of fiction. While some of the places are real, any resemblance to actual persons, living or dead is entirely coincidental.

Warning: sexual content. This book contains graphic imagery of men having sex together. And enjoying it. However, the story is primarily a romance. Don't be disappointed if you read pages and pages and pages without encountering acts, organs, or orgasms.

Dedication

For my Layapan dream girls,
Judith and Claudia

Acknowledgments

Sacred Hearts came out from Loose Id in December 2012. I'm happy to rerelease it for this Hanukkah season. I'm grateful to my Loose Id editor, Larke Butler, for her insightful suggestions on the initial book. And thank you to Jordan Castillo Price for her thoughtful reading and razor-sharp suggestions. Laurie Cheeley did a wonderful job proofreading this version. And Jordan Castillo Price created another spectacular cover. What a gift you all are.

In Mark Doty's poem "My Tattoo" he writes that the Sacred Heart represents education through suffering. That's a good description of this story. It is the third in the Tarnished Souls series — a set of standalone novels, each of which focuses on a different Jewish holiday. In most of the world, Hanukkah is a minor holiday. It's only celebrated in grand style in Israel and the United States — in Israel because it celebrates *a military victory and in the United States as compensation for Jewish children surrounded by Christmas. What Christmas and Hanukkah share (aside from the giving of gifts) are a celebration of lengthening days and the rebirth of the sun. As Hanukkah progresses we light more and more candles, symbolizing the return of hope in even the darkest times. For David, this story starts deep in his personal darkness — although he dreams of better things to come.*

Chapter One

It was eight o'clock on an otherwise normal Sunday night. I'd just started table four's entrées when my phone buzzed.

"David Schwartz?" Whoever she was, she sounded young.

"What can I do for you?"

Her voice was gravelly. "Rick Miller's your business partner, right?"

"Yes." And more. My stomach clenched. What had he done now?

"I'm a dealer at Fortuna's. I shouldn't be calling you, but I think you should come get him."

I opened my mouth to speak, but the phone went dead.

He was gambling again. *Fuck.*

Sunday nights I cooked alone. The only other chef, the one who worked with me on weekends and covered two midday shifts, was busy throwing our money away. I stared at the food sizzling on my grill. Across the room, Billy rinsed and loaded a short stack of dishes. The door opened behind me, and young Fred stepped in, his tray piled with vinaigrette-stained salad plates.

I waved him over. "We're closing early. Lock the door, turn off the outside light, and tell Charmaine to close as soon as these guys are finished."

Billy looked up from the dishes. He wiped his stubbled face with the sleeve of his shirt. "What's up, boss?"

I shook my head. "Something I need to take care of." I looked at the half-cooked food, grilling prawns, a couple of salmon fillets, and a steak. Getting them plated would take me five minutes, max. How much damage could he do in five?

Charmaine arrived at my elbow as I garnished the last of the plates. "Why are we closing?"

I hung up my chef's coat. "Rick's at Fortuna's."

All the sweetness drained from her honey-brown skin. "I thought he quit."

Anger rolled around in my gut like a roulette wheel. I shook my head. "Evidently he started again."

She gave a curt nod and began stacking plates up her arm.

I bolted out the back door and sprinted toward my car.

Fortuna's Wheel Poker Palace was a squat orange stucco building in a neighborhood in far northeast Portland, a couple of miles from the restaurant. It took me twenty minutes to get there. People clustered around the doorway, smoking. I showed the doorman my ID and stepped inside. Groups of grim-faced people sat around felted tables, their arms resting on the padded table edge as they fingered various-sized stacks of brightly colored chips. It was surprisingly quiet for a room full of people. Sounds fell and died on the red, white, and black carpet. Someone laughed from across the room, where a handful of men leaned against the bar. I scanned the tables until I spotted his lucky, straw cowboy hat.

As I got closer, I saw wisps of blond hair poking from beneath the brim. *Shit.* How long had he been sitting here losing our nest egg? I put a hand on his shoulder. Rick pushed his short stack of hundred-dollar black chips into the center of the table. *Shit.* Once they were out there, they couldn't be pulled back. The dealer, a young woman with raven hair, a rose tattoo on her shoulder, and sad eyes gave me one long glance before she dealt the cards. No one else at the table took cards. Tension shot through the stone-faced group, but I'd been here before with Rick. It didn't matter what the cards were. In the end he always lost. I hoped I could drag him away with something in his pocket. Our pocket. My father had been right. It was time to close the joint checking account. Again.

Rick had a three showing. He curled up the facedown card. An eight. He tapped the table. She tossed him an ace.

I closed my eyes. I heard Rick tap.

"Shit." It came out of him like breath.

I opened my eyes. The jack of hearts lay face up next to the ace, three, and upturned eight. Twenty-two. The dealer raked in Rick's chips.

My grip closed around his shoulder. "Come on, let's go home."

He looked up at me. "Hey, just in time. You got some scratch I can use?"

I shook my head. "Not today."

He shrugged, pushed back from the table, and grinned at his fellow players. "Next time."

The dealer focused on her other customers and snapped open another deck.

***

"What do you mean, you emptied the business account?" I stared at Rick across our kitchen table. It was after midnight. I smelled the day's cooking fumes on my clothes, in my hair. Rick looked handsome, contrite, and ready to be forgiven. Again.

He stared at the coffee cup he was passing back and forth between his hands. "I was so close. If I'd had a few more chips, I could have turned it around."

"You promised you would never gamble again. 'Not even a lottery ticket.' That's what you said when you begged me to trust you."

"I know." He leaned forward, his eyes ablaze. "But, this is it, Davey. I can feel it, like fire in my veins. My luck is right here."

"Clearly." I glared at him until he looked away. "How are we going to make payroll or pay the vendors? That money wasn't yours to throw away."

His gaze flicked to mine. His voice rose and fell like that of a thwarted two-year-old. "But if I win, we can get that new stove you want. Maybe take a vacation. I'm doing this for us."

The chair clattered to the floor as I stood. "That's bullshit. You didn't gut our business for us. And since when did you care about us having a vacation? Remember the Caribbean cruise we had to cancel because you gambled away our vacation fund? Christ, Rick, it's taken us three years to build up a safety cushion for the restaurant, and now we're back at square one. We'll need to stretch our credit to the limit to pay this month's bills."

He shifted in his chair.

"Tell me."

He cleared his throat. "Yeah, about that. I meant to tell you, but I thought I'd get it back right away."

I opened my mouth, closed it. My voice came out in a whisper. "The business equity loan?"

He nodded, his eyes fixed on the table.

"Our credit cards?"

He looked up at me from under those thick eyelashes I used to love.

My throat was closing up. I downed what was left of my orange juice before croaking out, "Do we have anything left?"

He pursed his lips, drummed his fingers, tapped his feet, shuffled his butt, and eventually shook his head. "But I'm gonna get it back. Plus a lot more. I tell you, my luck's—"

"Fuck your luck." I grabbed the table edge to keep myself from falling as my carefully constructed world fell apart.

The image of those four dinners I'd finished plating after the dealer called me floated into my head. What had they cost me? I pictured the stack of black chips. A hundred dollars each. Five minutes. Maybe three hands of blackjack. What did that add up to? My car payment? A week's payroll? If I'd let those dinners go, what would I have been able to keep?

I forced him to meet my gaze. His deep blue eyes had that pleading look that always got me. But not this time. I felt nothing but contempt for us both. The self-destructive part of me that kept drawing me back to Rick was as drained as our bank accounts. When I could speak again, I whispered, "Go. We're done. Leave the keys to the apartment, to the restaurant, and get out of here. I don't want to see you again."

I saw the beginnings of his protest. Something in my look stopped him. He stood and walked to the bedroom. I leaned against the table, listening to him pack. It didn't matter what he took with him. There wasn't anything worth having that he hadn't already stolen.

***

I woke with my heart pounding. In my dream, I'd been running from something big and terrifying. What it had been faded as I opened my eyes to take in the familiar walls of my bedroom, gray in the dim, dawn light. There'd been something else. Not scary, but beautiful. A man emerging from the waves. Light streamed from somewhere behind him, and I couldn't make out the details of his face, only that he was tall. Tall and thin with a halo of wild curls.

My pulse slowed, fear dissolving into sadness as I registered the open empty drawers and the gaping space in the closet where Rick's clothes used to hang. It was a bittersweet relief to have him gone. After all, I'd been lonely for a long time. I pictured the man from my dream holding out his arms. That's what I wanted—something deep, sweet, and real. *Right.* Now I was planning happiness with an imaginary lover.

I threw off the covers and sat on the edge of the bed. This wasn't the time to wallow in regrets or fantasies. I needed to face up to the wreckage I'd allowed Rick to make in my life and start picking up the pieces. The only thing to do was get up, make myself some coffee, and take a dose of reality.

There's a mind-numbing, free-fall feeling when every account is empty, every line of credit maxed.

After checking all our accounts online and confirming that we were beyond broke, I closed every last one of them. The last thing I needed was for Rick to figure out a way to get us further into debt. I called the lawyer Papa recommended. As a favor to my father, he agreed to squeeze me in before lunch.

***

The restaurant was dark and smelled of seared meat and floor cleaner. I jotted the janitor's name on my list of people

I needed to call so I could explain that no one was getting paid because I'd believed in my asshole boyfriend's so-called recovery. I should have known better than to trust him. Again. What's a relationship without trust? That thought was the sucker button in the middle of my chest that Rick knew how to push every time. I stood in the middle of my slaughtered little restaurant, my stomach clenching with anger. Damned if I'd trust him ever again.

It could have been worse. When we'd opened the restaurant, Rick had argued we should go big, with a huge, noisy kitchen full of chefs cranking out entrées by the dozen and an elegant dining room that could seat a hundred. I thought we should start small and eclectic. A few tables and a limited menu, open only for dinner. Done right, the place would seem exclusive, I'd said. And it was all we could afford. Since I'd had the good credit and written the business plan, I'd won.

Now I looked around at the dark blue walls covered in local art. I'd need to contact the artists so they could take their work home. I ran my hand along the back of one of the ancient chairs we'd bought at auction and spent long hours refinishing in the months before the restaurant opened. Covered with bright floral linens that always reminded me of Mexico, my ten tables sat ready for dinner. I straightened a crooked knife at one setting. Crisp white napkins folded like lilies marked each place. The sight usually made me smile as I imagined the beautiful plates of food to come. This morning it had me eyeing a bottle of good brandy beside the wine rack.

The cash register opened with a sigh. I thumbed the ones, fives, tens, and twenties. I knelt to open the safe. Sunday nights were slow, and we'd closed early, so I wasn't surprised that the blue deposit bag felt slimmer than usual. I pulled out the deposit slip, written in Charmaine's careful script. About six hundred. With the drawer, that meant I had less than a thousand dollars, which wouldn't make a dent in what I owed. Credit card receipts would be sucked into my void of debt, but there was some currency and a few checks I could cash. Reaching into the back of the safe, I retrieved the pink plastic box Rick had bought to hold spare rolls of quarters, dimes, nickels, and pennies. He'd drawn eyes and a snout on it and called it our piggy bank. Inside was thirty-seven dollars and fifty cents. I added the rolls of coins to my pile of cash and checks and stared at the box, which he'd presented to me with great ceremony on our opening night. I had a sudden urge to break the fucking thing, see it splinter under my heel. Instead I tossed it into the trash and gathered my paltry stack of money.

I left the drawer alone, slid the deposit into my jacket pocket, and started dialing phone numbers, calling in the troops for what promised to be the worst staff meeting ever. I got through to most and left messages for the rest. I went to the kitchen to continue my dismal inventory.

***

Abraham Klein had an office on the fifth floor of an ornate building in the historic district. It was furnished simply, with gleaming pine floors and upholstered wooden chairs. The view consisted of other old buildings, seen through ancient, double-hung windows. His secretary, a tall, thin woman with gray hair swept into a bun, waved me through. Abe stood to shake my hand with the same firmness and warmth as the last time I saw him, during the High Holidays—the only time I ever made it to Temple.

He gestured for me to sit. "Your father said something about money trouble?"

I nodded and cleared my throat, humiliation blooming in my gut. "My partner has a gambling problem."

Abe's brow wrinkled. "Business partner?"

I looked down at my white knuckles. "That too."

His chair creaked. When I looked up, he was peering from over tented fingers. "Does he… It is he?"

I nodded.

"Does he have access to your assets?"

I snorted. "He did. When I had assets."

"Ah. Show me."

I spread my papers out across his desk. After a few minutes, he looked up again. "I take it you've closed these accounts?"

I shrugged. "Too little, too late, but yes."

"And Mr. Miller"—he looked from the bank statements to my loan account balances—"why isn't he a co-borrower on these loans?"

It felt like a bottomless pit of shame was opening in my belly. "He, um, he wasn't a good enough credit risk."

Abe stared at me for a long moment. "What is the status of your relationship now?"

My head hurt. I rubbed at my temples. "It's over."

"Good." His sharp eyes were surprisingly kind. "Your options are limited, and I'm afraid the burden of debt falls directly on you."

I sighed.

He leaned back in his chair and contemplated me with a fatherly look. "If it helps, in my experience, people are only betrayed by the ones they're closest to."

I shook my head. "That's hardly comforting. Where do I go from here?"

***

The first place I went after meeting Abe was to an AA meeting. People nodded to me in greeting, and someone offered me a cup of coffee. In the ten years I'd been frequenting church basements, I'd been to good meetings and bad meetings and meetings that rocked my world, but I'd always walked out feeling better than I did when I sat down.

This was no exception. A guy with thirty days talked about facing jail time for a DUI, and I realized that closing a restaurant wasn't the worst thing in the world. An old-timer reminded us all to be grateful for what was working and to turn the rest over to our Higher Power. I took a deep breath and thought about that. I was healthy and still relatively young. Whatever the devastation Rick had wreaked in my life, it wouldn't last forever. By the time the meeting ended and I caught a bus back to the restaurant, I was determined to make it through this one long, hard, fucking, sucky day, even if it took going one hour at a time.

We opened at six, so I'd scheduled the staff meeting for four. How long could it take to tell eight people they were out of a job?

Charmaine arrived first. It was her night off, so she had the baby asleep in a sling across her chest. I was sitting at the table nearest the kitchen, filling out the first few pages of my bankruptcy paperwork.

She settled into a chair across from me. "This isn't good, is it?"

I shook my head. "He wiped us out. We're going under."

She closed her eyes. "When?"

I looked down at my inventory list. "Soon. We've enough food for a few days, maybe a week with some creative menu manipulation. But there's nothing for wages."

"Nothing?"

The door opened. Billy and Fred came in, trailed by the rest of the kitchen and waitstaff. They were laughing and talking until they spotted Charmaine and me sitting in depressed silence at the back of the room. The group formed a tight circle around us. They waited for me to speak.

Rigorous honesty. It was one of the first principles I'd learned in treatment. I'd been trying to practice it in all my affairs for ten years. Sometimes it was easier than others. I looked at their faces. Charmaine with her new baby. Billy, coming out of his own stint in rehab. Fred, whose mother had leukemia. People who depended on income from my restaurant to pay their rent, feed their families, and repay student loans.

I told them what I'd told Charmaine, that we were flat broke. Fred stared at me openmouthed. Billy jammed his hands into his pockets and shrunk into himself. Watching them, I felt a leaden mixture of guilt and sadness that made it hard to continue.

With an effort I took out the deposit envelope from the night before and pulled out eight small bundles of bills, each held by a paper clip. I handed one to each of them. "This is all I could salvage from last night's receipts. There's forty-seven dollars for each of you. It's all I've got. I'll start making calls tomorrow, see if anyone's hiring. I'm planning on staying open until the food runs out. If any of you are up for that, we can split the take each night until it stops making sense. If you're not interested, don't worry about it. Everyone's getting my highest recommendation. You've been a wonderful crew."

When I was done, there was silence. Charmaine wiped away a tear. A couple of the others started shrugging on coats. I pulled two bottles of wine from the shelf behind me. "I've got some work to do in back. You guys have a drink on me. For anyone who wants to stay and work, we'll open in an hour."

I went back to the kitchen and turned on some music. I didn't want to hear them deciding what to do.

After a while, Charmaine joined me.

"How's it look out there?"

Charmaine shrugged. "Most everyone's gone home to polish their résumés. Billy's helping Fred set up." She gestured toward the baby. "I can't afford to get a sitter, but I can go home and pick up her playpen if you like. Billy said she'd be fine in the corner by him."

"You don't have to do that." I stroked the soft hair on the baby's head.

She shrugged. "I was here your first night. Might as well be here your last." She gazed at me for a long moment, hand on her hip. "You know you deserve better than Rick, right? Give it time, honey, and the right man will come along." She turned and strode out the door.

I stared after her. The right man? After putting up with Rick for so long, I deserved a fucking saint. Except it was my own damned fault. I was the one who kept taking him back.

It was quarter to six when Charmaine returned, a folded playpen beneath her arm and an overstuffed baby bag over her shoulder. Billy babbled at the baby from his sink full of prep pans, and it occurred to me that he probably had grandchildren somewhere, left behind in his gutter-drunk days. Charmaine handed the squirming bundle to him while she set up the playpen in the corner, safe from the hot dishwasher spray. Billy gurgled up at the baby, who pumped her fists in the air in reply.

As Charmaine started out the kitchen door, I called, "Don't take credit cards. Checks and cash only, otherwise we'll never see the money."

She gave a curt nod and went to open the door.

***

Word got around by the second night, and we were slammed. People kept coming back into the kitchen to say how sorry they were to see us close. By the next night we had to reduce the menu offering substantially, and by Wednesday it was clear we had to close. After closing Wednesday night, I cooked us all the best dinner I could scavenge. I emptied the cash register, dividing everything we had into four neat piles. I sent the rest of the wine home with Charmaine and Fred, gave Billy my supply of soft drinks, and emptied the walk-in and the pantry into grocery bags for all three of them. I took one last look at my beautiful, airy restaurant before locking the doors and driving home.

I spent two days wheedling, and found part-time jobs for everyone on staff, although no one needed a chef. After that, it took two weeks and a giant garage sale to sell it all—the restaurant equipment, apartment furniture, sound system, my car. My life shriveled, until everything I owned fit into my two bags. The proceeds paid a week's severance for the staff and the flat fee for Abe Klein. I defaulted on debts to vendors, broke two leases—one on the apartment, one on the restaurant—all of which pretty much guaranteed I wouldn't be opening another place anytime soon. Good thing Portland had an excellent public transportation system, since I was about to be job hunting in a saturated market. Two years of cooking school, ten years of experience, three years running my own trendy place, and I'd be lucky to find a job as a greasy-diner short-order cook.

Chapter Two

I climbed out of the cab and stared at the split-level suburban for a few minutes before shouldering my backpack and wheeling my suitcase up the walk. You know you're a failure when you have to move back into your childhood home as an adult. For the second time.

The key was under the planter where my father always left it. I let myself in and lugged my belongings down the hall, past old pictures of my successful cousins—a New York finance lawyer, an English professor, two doctors, and another, a doctor's wife—and me, the only son, an unemployed chef and failed restaurateur whose finest achievement was sobriety. Not a small feat, but none of those twelve steps would pay the rent.

My room hadn't changed in the years since I last stayed, fresh out of treatment and shaky as an old man. It had taken me months to move out that time. Mom had poured gallons of chicken soup down me, as if alcoholism were a virus. It would be different this time, since I was sober and she was gone. Breast cancer hadn't responded to the soup either.

Thinking I should change and go for a run, I closed my eyes. Selling everything and giving up was exhausting.

***

I'm stumbling along a path by the ocean, searching for a safe place to lie down. I'm looking down at a pile of soft branches, a nest of some sort, and I start to sit. Then the sticks begin to writhe and hiss. Snakes. I scream. I'm running away, only there are snakes everywhere. The snakes slither, piles and piles of ropelike bodies slipping over each other. I'm sprinting down the beach, and the snakes are following me. And then he's there, with the light radiating from behind him, and he's walking through the waves toward me with his arms outstretched.

***

I woke to the familiar slam of the front door, and sat for a minute with my heart pounding. I'd been having these dreams every night since the restaurant closed. As always, the dream felt real. I shuddered. I could almost feel the snakes moving across my skin. And the guy, the one I thought of as my merman because I always dreamed him walking out of the sea with his arms held out—what was he, death? Some sort of angel? His body was beautiful, long, and lean. I couldn't see his face, but I was entranced by all that wild, dark curly hair. Familiar, and yet I couldn't think where I'd seen him. I shook my head. Probably an underwear model on a billboard I passed every day.

I heard my father moving around in the foyer. I'd meant to have dinner waiting for him, a peace offering to soften my latest degradation. Instead I'd slept away the afternoon. I rolled to sitting, slipped on my shoes, and went to face my disappointed father.

He looked the same, short, fat, and bald on top with a ring of Bozo-curly, white hair. It was how I would look if I didn't shave my head and run ten miles a week. We were handsome men, if you liked the swarthy, barrel-chested Eastern European Jew look. My father was five feet four inches tall. At five-eight, I towered over him, although he outweighed me by a good fifty pounds.

He sputtered hello, tried for a smile, shook my hand, slapped me on the back, and fell silent. There were many things Daniel Schwartz, owner of Schwartz Sporting Emporium, was good at. Dealing with emotionally fraught situations wasn't one of them.

"Hey, Papa." I patted his arm. "I'll make dinner."

Nodding, he thumped my back again. "Good, good. Look forward to it."

I turned toward the kitchen and let him escape to his room to change.

The refrigerator held a hodgepodge of beer, milk, a carton of eggs, half a withered onion, a hunk of cheddar, and condiments. The freezer above groaned with frozen dinners and ice cream. After shuffling through the canned goods— soup, olives, tuna—I leaned my head against the cupboard door. I could offer to shop and fill the larder, except I didn't want to part with my tiny store of cash.

A blast of TV came from the living room. Eggs, milk, cheese. I pulled open the flour drawer. The bag probably dated from Mom's last batch of cinnamon rolls two years before, but it would have to do. The utensils, bowls, and pans were where they'd been from the time I first stood at the kitchen counter, stirring chocolate chips into Mom's cookie batter. I felt better by the time the soufflé emerged from the oven, a perfect puffy counterpoint to my miserable life.

As he sat to dinner, Papa eyed the dome. He rubbed his hands together briskly and boomed, "This is great. Just great. No frozen food for me tonight. Not with my son the chef home."

I shrugged, embarrassed by how hard he was trying to cheer me up. "Cooking is the least I can do."

He settled a napkin on his lap as I scooped a generous portion of cheese soufflé onto his plate. After a minute, he added, as I knew he would, "I wish you'd stayed in school."

I scooped my own dinner, counted to ten, and sat down across from him. "Water under the bridge."

He shoved in a forkful of soufflé and grunted in approval. We ate silently for a few minutes.

Papa set down his fork and looked at me. "What are you going to do now?"

It was a really good question. I didn't know the answer. "I'll find something."

"You going to prosecute him?"

My fluffy creation turned to cement in my stomach. "I can't do that, Papa. We were…. He was…. I can't."

"What's Abe say?" He was on more comfortable ground now. My father wasn't afraid to take people who messed with him to court.

I had known we were going to have this conversation sooner or later. I'd been hoping for later. I set my fork down and pushed away my half-finished dinner. "Embezzlement is hard to prove among business partners. Especially when they live together and have an intimate relationship."

His lip curled in distaste. "Your mother never trusted him." He didn't have to say how he felt; Rick's financial instability had been a sticking point between us for years. Standing, he picked up his plate. He patted my shoulder, and I squeezed his hand as it lay there.

"You know you're welcome to stay as long as you need," he said as he continued to the sink.

"Thanks, Papa."

He cleared his throat. "No problem. Next week's Thanksgiving, and I'll have my own personal, live-in chef for it."

I laughed and started clearing the table. "Like every other year. Since when didn't I make you turkey?"

"Since before your mother got sick, God rest her soul." He smiled sadly and turned toward the living room.

"I can cook for more than two, you know," I called after him. "Any sexy widows you'd like to invite?"

"Maybe next year," I heard, before sound exploded again from the TV.

I cleared the table, scraped what was left of my soufflé into the trash, and filled the sink. I tried to lose myself in planning how to make Thanksgiving for two a festive meal. If I concentrated on food, I could almost ignore the pit of despair in my stomach. I had no restaurant, no job, no money, and no one to love, but I had a roof over my head.

***

The smell of exhaust roiled up around me as the bus pulled out of Pioneer Courthouse Square. I leaned back in the seat, rocking my feet to try to ease the ache. I unfolded the list from my pocket and crossed off three more restaurants. Not many left to try. Outside the bus, November was being ushered out by cold, slapping rain.

My cell buzzed. With any luck, I'd have a job before the phone company came to their senses and shut it off.

I checked the display. It was my old friend George. I hadn't heard from him in maybe a year, but we went way back. I worked to put some cheer into my tone. "Hi, George. How's it going?"

His was such a comforting rumble. "Hi, David. I hear rumors about you, man. You all right?"

I closed my eyes. Evidently the gossip train extended all the way to LA. "I've been better. Thanks for asking. How'd you hear?"

"Rick called."

I opened my eyes and focused on the pattern of rain pouring down the window. "Yeah, well, that's over."

George sighed. "Sorry, man."

"Don't be. It's for the best."

George grunted into the phone. "You know, we didn't want you to date him. Not after he sent my friend Pete running back to Wisconsin butt-broke and brokenhearted. Pete's doing great these days, by the way. So there's hope for you."

"Not your fault. Rick was supposedly cured, going to Gamblers Anonymous and all that." I wiped fog from the window with my sleeve. It left a dark stain of grime on my cuff. Guess my job hunting was over for the day. "I should have paid more attention. Why'd he call you?"

George snorted. "Actually he called Kenny, wanting to borrow money."

"Shit, George. That's embarrassing."

George chuckled. "Kenny's getting used to it. Write a successful screenplay, and suddenly you hear from a lot of old friends. Rick said you guys closed the restaurant?"

"Did he tell you he gutted it financially first?"

There was a silence on the other side of the phone. Eventually George said, "So where are you working?"

Rain streaked the bus window. "Nowhere yet. And I'm staying with my father. Depressing, right?"

"Maybe not. Am I remembering correctly that you were a Spanish major in college?"

"I dropped out my senior year, but yes."

"I've got an opportunity, if you're interested. Some scenes from Kenny's movie are being shot in Mexico. He's talked them into hiring my company to cook. We're down here already, and I'm up a creek. I need local help, but once I say, '*Buenos días*,' I've shot my whole load with Spanish. I need an assistant who can cook *and* talk. It's a short gig, but the pay is good. You up for it?"

I sat up straight in my seat. The young, white woman with elaborate dreads in the seat across from me looked up from her book. "Yes, yes. Of course, yes."

"Great. I'll book you a flight. Can you leave tomorrow? I need you right away. We only have a week before shooting starts. If everything stays on schedule, you'll be back home by New Year's." I could hear the grin in his voice. "It's a fucking gay mecca down here. We'll have a blast."

I thanked him profusely and hung up the phone. In cooking school George and I had buddied up the first day, both of us overwhelmed by the sheer eighteen-year-oldness of most of our fellow students. He was ten years older than I was, but even then, at twenty-six and newly sober, I felt ancient compared with my classmates. For George, cooking was a second career that followed a successful first one as an investment banker, while for me it was a lifeline, a path out of the stifling love of my parents' house, and a way to prove I wasn't going back to a gutter drunk's life. As I watched the wet winter landscape slide by the bus window, I wondered how much of this job was pure mercy. I decided to simply be thankful. And after years of forgetting about Mexico and of not taking a vacation, now I was going to spend December in Puerto Vallarta.

***

I left the rolling suitcase full of fleece, wool, and my good knives in my father's basement, and filled the backpack with my summer clothes. Downsizing had made it easy to pack.

Papa drove me to the airport. Pulling to the curb, he splashed through a puddle. Water arced onto the windshield, blurring my view of the terminal.

As I unbuckled my seat belt, he rested his hand on my shoulder. "You're a good boy, David."

I blinked, startled. "Thanks."

He opened the glove compartment, pulled out a wad of cash, and pressed it into my palm. "Take this. I don't want those movie people thinking you're a bum." I started to protest, but he reached across me and opened the door. "What am I going to do with it? It's not like I can take it with me."

"You're not going anywhere, Papa." I stuffed the cash in my pocket. Taking his money made me feel like a shit, even though I knew how much love came with it. "I'll pay you back as soon as I can."

"Sure, sure." He patted my arm. "Have a good time down there. And don't get yourself into trouble."

I smiled. "I'm already in trouble. But I know what you mean. Don't worry. My margarita days are over."

He nodded with plastic-dog-in-the-back-window eagerness. Overwhelmed with gratitude for how lucky I was to have a father like him, I kissed his cheek, then hurtled out of the car before either of us could do anything embarrassing.

I felt a surge of freedom as I stepped into the terminal. There was something about carrying everything on my back like a turtle that lifted my spirits. I dug my passport out of my pocket and got into line with all the other vacationers. A couple ahead of me was busy keeping a three-year-old entertained as he banged his toy sheep against the metal posts.

I stripped off my shoes, tossed them into a gray plastic bin, and shoved it and my pack through the x-ray machine. As I walked through the detector, it occurred to me that with one too many bad bets, Rick had blown up my life as neatly as any terrorist.

And I was walking away from the explosion. Even though George was only offering a temporary reprieve, it felt like a new beginning. I got onto the plane, feeling hope for the first time since Rick pulled the pin.

Chapter Three

And walked off into wet heat. My Pacific Northwest blood would require some serious thinning if I was going to survive this job. We funneled through a long yellow-and-orange corridor that dumped us into a huge white linoleum-floored room smelling of perfume, sweat, and tortillas. We separated into two streams to shuffle through black-corded labyrinths. At each wave of an officer, a nuclear family pod broke off and hurried toward the desk. Customs officers stamped each passport with three staccato bursts that sounded like a staple gun. I noticed a cluster of men, their hair gel, earrings, and gaits familiar, though their faces weren't. I watched as one was called to the podium. The others hesitated before joining, a nonnuclear family group.

Another long corridor, another almost empty room. I changed one hundred dollars of Papa's wad at the blue-and-white Cambio Banco booth and peed in a bathroom filled with the universal fake flower scent of cheap floor cleaner. I stepped through double sliding glass doors into a cacophony of "Excuse me, mister" and "Taxi?" and "What resort you staying at, mister?"

I walked quickly on until I heard a familiar squeal.

"There he is." Kenny rushed toward me. He was easy to spot in his red-and-pink Hawaiian shirt and straw fedora. George ambled behind, taller and much more subdued.

Back when we were in cooking school, George had dressed like what he was, an ex-banker. Now, after years of Kenny's guidance, he again looked like what he was, owner of one of the hippest catering companies in LA. And yet he still looked like George. Kenny might go in for hair gel and trendy sunglasses for himself, but he always dressed George in classic lines that accentuated his aging, surfer-boy good looks.

Standing in my khaki shorts and baggy tee, I felt like a Portland fashion refugee. Which might have been a fair description. Still, it had been a while since anyone looked happy to see me. I embraced them both.

"Honey, you're going to love this place." Kenny slipped his arm through mine. "It's a fagopical paradise."

George rested a hand on my shoulder. "How was your flight?"

"You must be starving. We'll stop for a fish burrito on the way. George discovered an amazing little hole-in-the-wall not far from here."

"Smoked mackerel burritos," George interjected. "The best I've ever had."

"Speaking of the best I've never had." Kenny waved to a dark man in a blue suit that looked way too heavy for the climate. "That's our driver. And before you say anything about his fabulous ass, his English is better than yours."

I shook the driver's hand and passed him my backpack, ignoring his purportedly fabulous ass.

Kenny sat in front, while George and I piled into the back of a battered blue sedan. The driver swung the car into traffic with a lurch that sent my heart pounding. Buses rumbled by, the smell of exhaust thick in the air. Out the window, the scenery looked like any other suburban landscape—big-box stores and hotels—except, of course, that all the signs were in Spanish, a language I'd been fluent in once. I'd meant to polish my very rusty skills by reading an Arturo Arias novel in the original on the plane but had fallen asleep instead.

At Kenny's direction, the driver parked the car in front of a concrete shack festooned with brightly colored posters of marlin and tuna. We piled out. The scent of grilled fish swept over me, and my stomach growled. We approached the counter.

"Burritos," a twentyish waiter explained hesitantly.

I opened my mouth to ask him questions and was incredibly grateful when Spanish spilled forth.

Kenny and George looked on, smiling and nodding like proud parents of a piano-playing four-year-old, while I ordered the burritos and the waiter and I made small talk. George fell into a chair at the nearest table, Kenny settled gracefully beside him, and I followed. Our driver took his lunch to the car.

I bit into the spongy flour tortilla filled with pungent fish, my first taste of Mexico since senior year in college, when I'd taken a semester abroad and fallen in love with a beautiful boy named Antonio. When he was gone, I stayed and drank my way through the spring semester, my non-graduation, and another full year before my parents found me and dragged me home. I didn't remember the food from back then. It was all a blur of dirty bars, home-brewed tequila, blowjobs involving brown-eyed boys, and back-alley vomiting. I must have eaten, though, since it was a year before I got rid of all the intestinal parasites, and two more before I sobered up.

Sober, in a sunny café with traffic roaring past behind me, I tasted the oily burrito. Better than anything I could remember, it was smoky and rich. Comparing it to an American fish taco would be like calling coq au vin roast chicken.

Kenny and George tried to fill me in on the movie, the director, and the male lead, a well-known actor Kenny claimed had slept with half the gay men in LA. As usual, Kenny did most of the talking, while George encouraged him with murmurs, nods, and tiny touches to his arm, his hand, his back, in their own private love language. Kenny was the vivid flower of their relationship, and George the rock he grew out of, or some such nonsense.

Years ago I met Rick at Kenny's house. Now, as I sat watching George and Kenny, it dawned on me that one of the reasons I'd fallen for Rick was because of how being around Kenny and George made me long for a relationship exactly like the one I was watching. Only Rick hadn't been Kenny, and I was no George. They'd warned me about Rick. I should have listened.

After lunch, the driver dropped us at a fancy hotel by the beach. Kenny kissed my cheeks and dashed inside so he could work on "a bathtub full of script changes."

"I'll walk you to your hotel." George smiled apologetically. "I'm staying here with Kenny and the rest of the important folks. I'm afraid they're housing crew farther inland."

I shouldered my pack. "Hey, I've been sleeping in my old room at my father's house. Papa's great, but anything's better than that."

"We'll walk along the ocean for as long as we can." George led me along a board walkway, one side of which was lined with open-air restaurants. On the other, a long white beach stretched to the ocean. Middle-aged couples in bathing suits strolled next to honeymooners, while flocks of laughing men wove in and out of the crowd. Vendors selling brightly colored food, baskets, and toys milled around.

A long fiberglass boat that looked like a rowboat on steroids nudged onto the beach. A tall figure jumped out and began helping the other passengers disembark. When everyone was off, he waved to the boat driver and strode toward us. He looked familiar, but I couldn't place where I'd seen him before. He moved like a sea creature, all sleek muscles, and grace. He glanced toward me. Our eyes met, and I felt a shock, the kind a lamp must feel when you plug it in. Breath became difficult. My mouth went dry. My foot hit something on the boardwalk, and I stumbled.

George caught my arm. "Are you okay?"

The stranger took in George's touch on my arm and looked away. Before I could speak, he disappeared into the crowd.

George followed my gaze. "This is a surprisingly small town. Unless he leaves today, you'll see him again."

That was something to pray for.

We walked along narrow streets away from the beach. The sidewalk was a conglomeration of cobbled areas, tile, bricks, and cement. As we moved inland, the shops lining the streets changed from pharmacies and stalls hawking plastic tourist kitsch to grocery and clothing stores. We passed street vendors selling tacos, roasted chickens, and sliced fruit in plastic cups.

Even though the hotel was only six blocks from the beach, it felt urban. Modern art hung on rich orange walls. The rooms were arranged in a circle around the inner courtyard. As cheap hotels went, it was pretty classy. The desk clerk handed me my key and a remote for the TV. George waited in the lobby while I walked the three flights of stairs. Mine was a small room. A bed, bureau, and sink filled the space. I opened the door to a tiny bathroom with a shower and toilet. At least I wouldn't have to share.

I dropped my pack on the bed and sprinted down the stairs. All the way down I could hear George in a stilted conversation about the weather with the desk clerk. They both looked relieved when I arrived.

Out on the street again, George shook his head. "You see, that's why you're here. There's no way I can negotiate for food in a foreign language."

"So tell me what you want me to do." I inhaled the thick, wet air, so different from home.

George started walking toward the beach. He had long West Coast American legs and a brisk stride. I had to trot to stay close enough to hear what he was saying. "Right now there's only the director, producer, and Kenny to feed, so we've been sampling the restaurants. But starting next week, we'll have a whole crew. I don't like buying food through middlemen. I need you to line up our suppliers. We're feeding five hundred people for two weeks. It's a big enough operation that they'll deliver, but you're my quality control guy. I'll show you around the catering truck later. It's parked by the hotel where we left Kenny. We'll need to hire a local crew to help out, and you'll be in charge of them since I can't communicate."

"What's the cuisine?"

He shrugged. "Mostly movie-star, fat-free, low-carb California 'lite,' but with a Mexican flair, which mostly means adding salsa, guacamole, and corn tortillas. We'll need tons of fresh fruit, veggies, chicken—preferably without the feathers—skim milk, if you can find it, that sort of thing. And, of course, we'll need to cater to every kind of diet there is, from paleo to low fat to spinach and cottage cheese. There's a list of who eats what in the trailer."

"Budget?"

"Low-budget Hollywood style is going to be high budget here. See if you can get an idea of the prices locals pay for this stuff, and don't let them charge us more than fifty percent over that." He gestured to a man selling an armful of necklaces. "People here make in a year what our director spent last night on dinner. Overpaying will create goodwill, but getting gouged won't make the producers happy."

He pushed open the hotel door and led me into an air-conditioned lobby. He punched the elevator button.

"Thanks for this," I said as I stepped into the carpeted box.

"No problem." He pressed a button, and the door closed us in. He looked closely at me. "You know, I'd forgotten that Mexico was where you—"

I stopped him. "Don't worry about it."

He cleared his throat and drew a piece of paper out of his pocket. He held it out. "I, uh, I got the schedule for AA meetings in Puerto Vallarta. There's a meeting place around the corner from here."

"Thanks. I'm not sure I'll have time." I took it and stuffed it in my shirt pocket.

He patted my arm. "Make time if you need to."

I nodded. The elevator door opened, rescuing me from the need to go on.

***

George gave me a cheap cell phone and the keys to a dented, red scooter, perfect for negotiating narrow cobbled streets. I plotted sites on a map and headed first to an operation listed as a fruit wholesaler, which turned out to be a guy with a beat-up blue pickup full of locally grown oranges, papayas, mangos, and bananas. He assured me he could deliver as much as we wanted. I signed him and two more like him. In the hills above the city, I found an avocado farm, where the youngest son agreed to deliver a bushel a day.

Organic salad greens took some finding, as did sources of local eggs. We would need a lot of chickens to reliably feed a movie crew. I negotiated with a couple of local entrepreneurs to purchase and deliver snapper, mackerel, and shrimp straight off the boat. The *tortillaria* I liked best was a clean white hole-in-the-wall on a bumpy side street in the Romantic district. Giant bags of *masa harina* lined one wall. An old woman stood on a step stool, feeding dough into a giant metal machine. Her daughter dropped a fresh, hot corn tortilla in my hand for tasting. It melted in my mouth, so different from the cardboard tortillas available in the states. I ordered thirty kilos a day, starting on Sunday, and drove off with a half kilo for myself.

Memories of Antonio flooded me as I drove the streets of Puerto Vallarta. I was twenty-one. He was two years younger, with dark eyes so sweet I never wanted to look away. I thought we'd be together forever. He used to drill me, pinching my nose, holding my tongue, making me repeat words and sounds until I lost my American accent. Eventually, between my dark coloring and my decent Spanish, people had mistaken me for a native. In the intervening years, while I buried the memory of

Antonio so deep that I almost forgot, I'd lost some fluency, but as the day went on, my tongue and heart started remembering.

Kenny and George had a dinner meeting with the producers and director, so I was on my own for the evening. I bought a couple of shredded beef tacos from a street cart. As I walked the uneven sidewalk, the night felt cool after the hot day. I found an Internet café, paid my ten pesos, and wrote an e-mail to Papa, letting him know I was okay. My in-box was full of retail advertisements, pleas from non-profits, and something from Rick. My finger hovered over the Delete button for a few seconds. But I wasn't that strong. My stomach knotted as I opened it.

I'm sorry, David, about everything. You've gotta know I did it for us. Really. I love you, and I want to work it out. Call me.

There was no way I'd call him. I'd been down that road before, closing bank accounts only to open them again. He had talked me into trusting him one too many times. He'd tell me he was sorry, he loved me, he was never going to gamble again. *"How can I prove that I'm recovering,"* he'd ask, *"if you don't trust me with money?"* Fuck him. I was done being his patsy. I hit *delete*.

Outside, the air had cooled, and I shivered. I wasn't ready to cocoon myself in my room, so I shoved my hands in the pockets of my shorts and walked, turning onto side streets, past open stores and closed ones, and squeezing around food stalls and past construction. After Antonio, I told everyone that true love was too painful. A pretty face and a nice ass, that's all I said I wanted. And with Rick, I got all that and a lot of headache. But not heartache. Was this nothingness he gave me better than grief? It felt like I was floating in a temporary Mexican dream. Eventually, I'd need to wake up and start my life again.

Chapter Four

The first text on my new, Mexican phone was from Kenny.

It's Saturday, 1st night Hanukkah. Going dancing. Wanna come?

Some years Hanukkah lines up perfectly with Christmas. This wasn't one of those. When I was a kid, I loved it when Hanukkah fell early in December because it made all my Christian friends jealous. Of course, that changed a few weeks later when their stockings were filled and we were eating Chinese takeout while I played with my already broken toys.

I pulled out the tin Hanukkah menorah Papa had stuffed into my backpack along with a box of candy-colored candles, and set them up for the first night—one scrawny-looking yellow twist of wax on the far end of the menorah and a pink one in the center for the shammes, the candle-lighting candle. I balanced the whole thing on the windowsill, lit them, and whispered the blessing. I curled up on the bed to watch them burn down. It wasn't my favorite holiday, crammed as it was with memories of loss, but I did it every year, if only in remembrance. Antonio had loved the idea of Hanukkah. I remembered his eyes sparkling in the light of our half-filled menorah on the fourth night a long time ago.

Rick gave extravagant presents and expected the same in return. And I'd told myself that the reason I always celebrated Hanukkah alone was I couldn't afford to buy something for Rick for two holidays in a row, especially if one of them lasted eight nights. But as I sat in a small hotel room in Mexico, watching the candles burn, I realized that I'd been protecting the holiday, like a wound I'd poke gently every year to see how much it still hurt. This year the memory of Antonio felt both closer and farther away, and I was surprised to find myself smiling into the flickering light.

When the candles sputtered out, I stood up and started getting ready to go. Years ago, I started shaving my head, after a guy I was dating pointed out my growing bald spot. I was on my knees with his dick in my mouth at the time. The next day I went to the barber and had it all taken off. Now I lathered up with shaving cream, and shaved my head and face. I climbed out of the shower, toweled myself dry, and rubbed oil into my scalp until it gleamed, and rummaged through my tiny cache of clothes, looking for something dance-worthy. The best I could come up with was a snug black tee and a clean pair of jeans. In the back of my mind was the image of that familiar-looking guy I'd seen on the beach. I still couldn't place him, but whoever he was, I hoped I'd see him again.

Kenny and George met me in the lobby. They looked fabulous, of course. They led the way through the night streets toward the club. The electronic thrum and pulse grew louder as we neared it. A few guys milled around the entrance. Inside, it was smoky and dark. A cluster of men moved together on a dance floor. Another group hung by the bar. Christmas lights were everywhere. Hanukkah in Mexico seemed to be slipping by unnoticed. George brought a round of drinks from the bar. Kenny set his down on a table and sauntered onto the dance floor, pulling George in his wake. I found a wall to lean against and took in the scene.

The crowd was mostly gringos, although there was a smattering of slim, young Mexicans. Couples and groups danced, or at least bounced, to American music played by a Mexican DJ. This early in the evening there didn't appear to be too many guys seriously cruising. The club was filled with exuberant vacationers drinking too much, but laughing as they went.

I took a short sip of the too-sweet cola. It had been a long time since I'd been single. I watched the men on the dance floor. The music throbbed like a pulse.

I turned, and there he was. Light shone from behind so that his face was in shadow—the man from my dreams, my merman. I stared, barely breathing. It was him—tall, lean, his dark, curly hair untamed. Then he moved, and the halo of light turned into a naked light fixture, and his features resolved into the straight lines and planes of the guy from the beach, looking even better than he had when I first saw him. I blinked, trying to reconcile the merman and the man. Of course the beach guy couldn't be the merman from my dreams. That was impossible. But there he was, looking exactly like the man who kept emerging from the water whenever the snakes or spiders or bats threatened me.

I willed him to look my way, and eventually he did. That same shock coursed through me when our eyes met. My whole body responded. He straightened as if he felt the same pull. It was like getting swept up in a current, a riptide. He took a step toward me, and as if in a dream, I moved toward him. When our hands touched, I knew where the night would end. He let me lead him onto the dance floor.

He walked beautifully but danced like a fifteen-year-old trying to find the rhythm. Even awkward, he was gorgeous, all muscle and long bones. I danced closer, our bodies a whisper away from each other, near enough for me to bask in his heat. I looked up into his eyes and stopped breathing when I saw the hunger in his gaze. As if of their own accord, my hips pulsed forward, and I brushed my hardening cock against his. He caught his lower lip between his teeth. Someone bumped me from behind. I looked around and saw George giving me a thumbs-up before he pulled Kenny close and danced away. When I turned back to my companion, he nodded toward the door. I took his hand and followed him out into the night.

Outside, our hands dropped. I wedged mine in my pockets to keep from touching him as we walked silently along narrow streets and down to the beach. The moon lit the beach and sent sparkles of light careening off the waves. He bent to pull off his sandals and roll up his pant legs. I did the same. He looked down at me, his eyes dark green in the moonlight. He took my hand again. Blood rushed to fill my cock as he led me down the beach and toward the looming darkness of a rock wall. His hand was warm in mine. Cool sand squished between my toes. We walked toward the moon and into the surf. A cold wave crashed over my feet. Sand spilled from under my heels as it withdrew. We waded through surging water around the edge of the cliff. I could barely make out a short stretch of beach ahead of us, hemmed by cliffs on either side. My mystery man's hand tightened around mine as he pulled me forward, onto the beach. I splashed the last few feet, hurrying toward the moment I could wrap my hands, my tongue, my body around his.

He leaned back against the cliff. His body felt as spare and long as I had imagined. His mouth tasted like salt and spice. I braced myself against the cliff, my grip slipping on wet moss as he ran his hands from my shoulder blades to ass and back. My nose filled with the smell of ocean. I pressed against him, rubbing the hard line of his cock with my own. He squeezed my ass, holding me steady as he thrust against me, his tongue in my mouth like a promise of what could be. I tangled my fingers in his curls and opened farther to his tongue. He groaned into my mouth and pulled me up against him. The crashing waves muffled the sound of our breath, but I felt his chest rising, falling in quick bursts. I reached between us and unclasped his belt. He groaned again, falling back against the cliff as I unzipped his pants and slid my hand in to touch the tight, hot skin of his cock. I wrapped my hand around him and pulled. He broke our kiss with a gasp. I kissed his neck and started to drop to my knees, but he stopped me by snaking his hand into my pants and clasping me. I unfastened my jeans to give him room and fell back into the kiss, into the feel of his hand and his cock.

Above the sound of the ocean, I heard distant music. It felt like we were hidden in a secret cove. He stroked me in rhythm with the waves. I matched his pace and felt his breath against my cheek. I thrust into his hand. He held me as tightly as if I were in him entirely. His cock in my hand made my mouth water. It felt like sparklers flew through my veins, his touch igniting every nerve ending. A fire curled up from my toes, rushing through me like I was drought-bleached brush. He cried out. I felt him spill across my hand, and I was coming in wave after wave of desire.

I held him for a moment after, pulling away as an awkwardness descended between us like a curtain. I glanced away as I wiped my hands on my jeans and buttoned up. When I looked up, he was adjusting his pants, his gaze on the sand at our feet.

I cleared my throat. "Um, that was…" I trailed off, uncertain how to finish the sentence. *Great? Spectacular? Unusually good for a pickup? The first sex I've had with someone new in years, and I'm not sure what to do now?*

He glanced up and nervously stuck out his hand. "I'm John."

His voice, deep and resonant, sent shivers through me. I stared at him a minute before shaking the hand that had just stroked my dick. "David. Nice to meet you."

He squeezed my hand, and that current of connection shot through me again. John dropped my hand like it burned him. He kicked at the sand for a moment while I flailed around for something to say.

His gaze flicked up to meet mine. He shrugged awkwardly, turned, and sprinted into the waves. I watched openmouthed as he rounded the corner of the boulder and disappeared from sight. It had been a long time since I'd picked someone up, but I didn't remember anyone ever leaving so abruptly. Or shaking my hand after sex, for that matter. That was weird, but Fuckin' A, the guy was hot. Too late, I realized I hadn't gotten his number or even his last name.

A breeze picked up, and I shivered. I stared out at the ocean, cursing my dating ineptitude. Eventually, I waded around the cliff and up the beach to find my shoes and make the long, lonely walk back home.

***

The next morning, George and Kenny met me for breakfast at a café on the beach to savor our last full day before shooting started and the hungry hordes arrived.

As soon as I was within hearing distance, Kenny called, "Don't you look like a happy boy? I take it you had a good time with Mr. Tall-Dark-and-Handsome?"

I nodded to the waiter gesturing at me with his coffeepot and sat before answering. "It was…" I paused, unsure of how to describe my evening: Magical? Romantic? Amazing? Hot? "…nice."

Kenny frowned. "Visits to your great-aunts are nice, darling."

"No, it was good." I picked at the plastic edge of my menu. "It ended strangely. He, um, he sort of ran away."

George looked at me over his coffee cup. "You going to see him again?"

The server appeared, and I waited to answer until after he took our order. "I'd like to, but he left before I could get his number." I cleared my throat. "Here's the weird thing. I've been dreaming about a man I've been calling my merman for weeks, and I swear he looked exactly like John, the guy last night. Well, I mean his body did, anyway."

Kenny's eyebrows rose. "A merman, like half man, half fish, and all danger? That fellow last night may not have danced well, but it looked like he had two legs."

I shook my head. "No. I only call him a merman because he comes out of the sea. But it's impossible for someone you dream about to be real, isn't it?"

George reached across the table and patted my arm. "You've been under a lot of stress lately, David. It's not surprising you're having odd dreams. But it isn't healthy to make yourself believe a pickup is the man of your dreams."

Kenny added, "Especially if they shoot and run."

George squeezed my forearm. "Don't let your imagination get away from you."

I thought I detected pity in the look they exchanged, so I changed the subject. "So what's it going to be like catering the movie?"

George leaned back and crossed his ankles. "It'll be wild. It's pretty much eighteen-hour days starting at three a.m. They eat in shifts. Breakfast goes until an hour or so before lunch, which ends around four. They're on a tight schedule, and some of the cast and crew are nervous about eating at local restaurants, so we're scheduled to cook dinner most nights. Don't expect to be done before eight or nine at night."

"You do this all the time?" I can live without sleep as well as the next guy. But not forever.

"The pay's good, and there's usually at least a couple of weeks between gigs." He considered me. "It's production cooking—less boutique than you're used to. We'll set out buckets of food, most of which won't get eaten, but all of it needs to look really good, taste fresh, and change every couple hours."

"That sounds wasteful." I waved away a woman trying to sell me one of the beaded necklaces weighing down her arm.

He shrugged. "We can refashion some of it, so that today's chicken wings become tomorrow's chicken tacos, and send the rest home with the crew. But you're right. It's not a thrifty operation."

Kenny shook his head. "I keep telling him he needs to hire someone to take the morning shift. Three a.m. is too damned early."

George fiddled with his cup. "Do you know what you're going to do when this is over?"

I stared out at the ocean. "Not a clue."

"Weather's great in LA. I might be able to find you something."

I looked at him. He was gazing into his cup. "Thank you. That's really sweet."

It was good to have friends.

***

The next morning the production slammed into me and left me breathless. Kenny was right. Three a.m. was way too early.

The trailer was a long, thin metal box with no windows and only enough room for a counter, steam table, six-burner stove, giant oven, large griddle, two cooks, and a dishwasher. It was like working in a tin box. It was hot and would be unbearable if the air-conditioning ever failed. We set up a prep area under an awning spread between the trailer and a smaller refrigerated truck. Four women washed and chopped fruits and vegetables, which were ferried in to us on large platters carried by teenage boys.

George put me in charge of translating both his words and his ideas to three shifts of women used to running their own kitchens. I organized the waitstaff and motivated dishwashers. It was more people management than I was used to. Payroll for my old restaurant topped out at a dozen, and that included the janitor, our bookkeeper, Rick, and me.

Following Kenny's directions, I sautéed, baked, and fried in a continuous flow from meal to meal. I felt like an army cook as I slung food onto platters for Kenny to arrange and garnish before he handed them to the waiters to carry out. My feet and back ached by the time we wrapped up our first day. Suddenly a three-week run sounded like a really long time.

Tired as I was, I felt too keyed up to go straight back to the apartment. My thoughts kept circling back to the merman. John. I hoped his quick exit didn't mean what Kenny seemed to think it meant, that the other night had been destined to be a one-time thing. As I wandered, I hadn't known where I was headed, but wasn't surprised when the club emerged around the next turn. I listened to the music for a while before I paid the cover and stepped inside. He wasn't there. I leaned against a wall and watched men dance, some close as breath, others at a distance. The door opened and closed and opened again, and still he didn't show.

He couldn't be literally the man in my dreams. That was ridiculous. George was right. It was a sign of how stressed I'd been, and how alone, that I was making cosmic connections out of a casual hookup. I walked down to the beach. Moonlight danced on crashing waves. The sand stretched out, lonely in the stark light. I turned onto the boardwalk. Couples of all shapes, ages, and genders strolled past. Blues and jazz spilled out of open-air bars. It was cold and late, and I was too old to daydream about my one-night stands. I turned inland, heading toward my room, another candle in the menorah, and an early morning wake up call.

Chapter Five

At least I had a job. And over the course of the next few days, we all got better. I learned everyone's name, and the Mexican crew learned to ask me questions one at a time. I learned to pace myself, and they learned to slice julienned potatoes and radish flowers. George even learned a little Spanish. By midweek we had developed a rhythm that allowed me to take short breaks. Without them, I'd be spending a month in Mexico without ever seeing the sun.

The filming took place mostly on the beach. The waitstaff trotted trays mounded with food down the boardwalk to a tent set up to feed extras, crew, and stars alike. Our main challenges were to make sure the buffet was stocked, the cold foods iced, the hot foods hot, and to keep sand out of everything.

It was weird seeing people in person after years of seeing them up close on the screen. The female lead was shockingly thin. As far as I could tell, she lived on celery and mineral water. It occurred to me that I was watching her starve to death.

The famous male lead had a firm, strong jaw, great hair, and was about my height, shorter than I'd expected. He had all sorts of special dietary needs—no gluten, no dairy, protein shakes made exactly to a recipe taped above the blender in the trailer. He started drinking tequila every afternoon around three, managing to avoid getting totally hammered until shooting stopped for the night. Late one afternoon, he whispered sloppily that my lips would look great around his cock. His booze breath sent tingles of memory through me. I saw him eyeing one of the teenagers carting food from the prep area toward the kitchen. The next day I assigned a sixty-year-old Mexican man to serve him.

The fifth night of Hanukkah was always the hardest. It was on that night a long time ago that I set the menorah on the windowsill next to a wrapped package and waited for Antonio, who never came home. For years afterward, I'd worn my present to him—a tooled leather bracelet. I took it off when Rick and I got serious, telling myself it was time. Now that I thought about it, moving in with Rick had been more about giving up than moving on. Here I was, back in Mexico, watching the candles burn and remembering what it felt like to be in love. I sat on the bed, my chin resting on my knees, until the last flame flickered out, leaving me alone in the dark.

***

After work on Thursday night, I strolled along the riverbank marketplace, where merchants called out to tourists, offering goods "almost free." In a small shop under the bridge, I found a tin merman with wild, dark hair and greenish eyes. I didn't haggle over the price. It was crazy to obsess like this over a one-night stand. I stared into the painted eyes of the merman and caressed his bare chest. I tried to remember exactly what my dream man had looked like, but all I could see was John's angular silhouette.

I wandered out of the market and sat in the square in front of the cathedral. A cool breeze blew in from the ocean. I watched tourists of all sorts strolling along the Malecon, a long boardwalk that spanned the central Puerto Vallarta beach. As the night wore on, families gave way to couples. Watching people walk by hand in hand only added to my sense of isolation. The thought of my years wasted with handsome, thieving Rick made me sad, and Antonio's ghost was cold comfort. I walked home and hung the merman next to my bed. It was the sixth night of Hanukkah. After I lit the candles and watched them burn, I found myself walking back to the club. Almost a week had gone by with no sign of him.

***

I could smell it. I could taste it. Hot, amber, delicious, it ran down the merman's body like gold, and I was licking, slurping, sucking it down, tequila warming my chest like love. I looked up into his gorgeous face, watched his wild, dark curls sway as I gulped from the waterfall of alcohol cascading down him. His face morphed, his hair turned from dark to light, and he was laughing at me, his face twisted with disdain beneath a lucky cowboy hat. The tequila turned to piss.

***

I woke sweating, the loss of ten years of sobriety like an ache in my chest. I opened my eyes, relief washing through me when I found myself in my hotel room. I made out the shape of my Hanukkah menorah on the windowsill and remembered lighting the candles and whispering the blessings to myself, alone and sober in Puerto Vallarta.

I sat up and switched on the light. Under a stack of papers on the bedside table, I found the meeting list George had given me my first day. As he said, there was a meeting place near the set. I checked my watch. I needed to be at work in two hours. The next meeting, called the Sunrise Group, was at five. I hadn't felt this close to a drink in years. If I started work early, maybe I could get enough ahead to duck out for an hour, because God knew I needed a meeting.

I was running on almost no sleep. Every cell in my body screamed as I hoisted myself out of bed. A shower and shave helped. I was going to need a lot of caffeine. With any luck, the huge pot of bad coffee would be an AA meeting tradition that translated across the border.

It was pitch-dark as I waved to the hotel clerk and stepped outside. A bus rambled past, populated by sleepy-looking locals on their way to wherever people went in the middle of the night. I heard a truck in the distance. Other than that, the streets were quiet, eerie after the daytime bustle.

I used my key to open the trailer, slammed on the lights, and shrugged into my chef's coat. With only me breathing the air, the trailer was slightly less claustrophobic than usual. By the time George and the rest of the crew arrived, I had things well under way.

George frowned at me. "Have you been here all night?"

I shook my head. "I came in early. I need to be somewhere between five and six. That okay with you?"

He stared at me for a while and shrugged. "Didn't you tell me Juanita used to be a breakfast cook? She can cover for you. Make sure she knows what to do ahead of time, since I can't tell her."

***

The AA club was identifiable from a distance by the cluster of people outside smoking. A woman and two men put out their smokes and went into the building. As I neared the place, a tall, thin man in a worn tie-dyed tee stubbed out his cigarette and smiled at me.

"Here for the meeting?" His accent called up the image of mint juleps and sweet potato pie.

I nodded. "David, alcoholic."

He held out his hand. "Welcome, David. I'm Ty, grateful, recovering addict and alcoholic at your service. You down here visiting?"

I shook his hand. "I'm here for a few weeks working for the movie people."

"You got a phone? Can I see it for a minute?" I dug out my phone and passed it to him, figuring the production company could spare a few phone minutes if the guy really needed to make a call.

Ty opened the phone and started punching keys. He passed it back to me. "Now you have my number. It's good to have a local contact, in case you need to talk."

I stared at him. Nobody's that forthright in Portland.

He grinned. "Don't worry. I'm not trying to pick you up. My girlfriend would flat-out kill me. But everyone could use a friend."

I nodded. "Um, thanks. Just so you know, I am gay."

He shrugged. "I'm from Alabama, but that don't mean I'm a redneck. Come on. The meeting's gonna start real soon."

He led me inside where a small group of tired-looking addicts and alcoholics clustered in a dark room beneath posters reminding us to LET GO AND LET GOD, EASY DOES IT, and to take it ONE DAY AT A TIME. The tension in my chest eased. My life might be a mess, but it had been worse, and it would get better. I poured a cup of acrid-smelling coffee and found myself a seat.

Chapter Six

We managed to get done early on Saturday, the last night of Hanukkah. After work, Kenny and George took me out to a fancy dinner on the beach. We ate duck mango tacos and papaya-encrusted bluefin tuna at a table on the beach, our bare feet burrowing into the sand. It felt decadent in the sweetest way. Later, they wanted to go dancing. I almost begged off—I can only survive so many nights without sleep—but going to the club didn't seem such a lonely hope with the two of them along. Besides, as I watched Kenny and George on the dance floor, I started to believe again in true love. They always had that effect on me.

I felt him before I saw him. Like a tingle on my spine. I turned. He stared into my eyes. We didn't bother dancing. I followed him down to the beach, his hand hot and hungry in mine. An overcast sky darkened the scene. We edged along the cliff, and as a wave hit my foot with a cold splash, I was surprised to see him produce a flashlight. The round yellow beam bounced across waves and rocks as we circled the end of the point, heading to our secret cove.

Blood was pounding in my temples as I watched his shoulders swing with the rhythm of his steps. I unsnapped the top button of my jeans to ease the pressure against my cock. I thought about unzipping them entirely but reconsidered when I pictured myself walking up the beach with a protruding prick bouncing before me. Might be too creepy. Maybe next time I could convince him to come to my place.

Firm sand beneath my feet, a step, another, the flashlight clicked off, and he turned. He was probably four inches taller than I was. In the darkness his face was all planes and shadows, his eyes dark ovals holding my gaze. His lips curved. He ran his hand over my scalp, and I arched into him. I heard his breath catch, and his mouth was on mine. I opened to the heat of his tongue. He held me by the back of my neck, his other arm wrapped around my waist. I slid my hands down to cup his ass. Even through his clothes I felt the flex of his muscles, and longed to smell his skin away from the sea and to feel the flesh of his ass beneath my hands and tongue.

He turned us and pressed me against the cliff. I'd be peppered with marks from the pointy edges of rocks in the morning, but for the moment, there wasn't enough room in my mind for anything other than his tongue, his skin, and his cock as it rubbed across mine through our clothes.

His hands went to my jeans. His tongue found the sweet spot on my earlobe, and I pushed into him. He ran his hands under my tee. His hot fingers on my skin as he caressed my ribs contrasted with the cool night air and sent shivers through me. He sank to his knees, and I leaned into the rock face, releasing into the feel of his tongue on my chest and belly. Fingers found my nipple and squeezed, sending bolts of excitement that made my cock bob against his chin. I heard the crackle of plastic and felt the slow roll as he smoothed a condom onto me. Clearly a safety-conscious guy.

And then through the latex, his tongue. His mouth. My cock. I held still as he engulfed me in warmth. He drew back, and cold tickled my shaft. Again he warmed me, and again the air cooled. The smell of wet moss rose as I clutched at the cliff. I curled my bare feet in the sand. I touched his head, and his hair beneath my fingers was miraculously soft. In the dark all I could see was the outline of his head moving up and down, and a flurry of movement below as he took his own cock in hand. I wanted it to last forever. I tried to concentrate on the sound of breakers crashing against the shore, of distant traffic, the electric beat of a bass guitar somewhere far away. I focused on wet sand between my toes, the points of rock digging into my back, anything to keep from giving in to the ravenous swell. And yet it came, sweeping over me like the tide. I heard his breath change, felt him stiffen, imagined him spilling onto the beach, and I abandoned myself to the wave, crying out as I gushed into the condom.

I settled against the cliff, catching my breath. He stood and shook the sand from his pants as he adjusted his clothing. My papa taught me not to litter, so I zipped up and stuffed the wadded condom in my back pocket.

John and I stood looking at each other in the moonlight.

I cleared my throat and thrust my phone toward him. "Can we trade numbers?"

He stared at my phone. He opened his mouth and shut it again. After a moment he shrugged. "I don't... I can't."

"Right." I shoved my phone into a front pocket and looked out at the ocean. Nothing like rejection to spoil that post orgasmic glow.

John's hand closed around my arm. When I turned to look at him, he was holding out a slip of paper and a pen. "Please write down your number for me."

It was hard to see his expression in the dark, and I couldn't tell whether he was humoring me. I scribbled my number on the paper, which he slipped into a pocket before turning to go.

He leaned down awkwardly and kissed the top of my head. As I followed him around the boulder and watched him sprint up the beach, I wondered if he'd call.

***

The Malecon, the walkway along the beach, was a wonder, with sculptures erupting out of the sidewalk every few hundred feet and vendors of all sorts strolling among the tourists. Early in the morning, before the sun heated the day, people of all stripes walked dogs, jogged, and strode in chatty groups. Before shooting had started, every morning I'd strapped on my shoes and run down to the beach, up the Malecon, and back through town, usually stopping for breakfast at a cheap restaurant near the cathedral.

Since the long days had begun, I hadn't had time to run. Always an optimist, I'd stuffed a bag of running gear in the back of a cupboard in the trailer. The morning after I gave John my number was the first time I got a break early enough to go for a run before the heat got too overwhelming. My feet pounded the pavement with a satisfying slap as I passed retirees in tracksuits and couples walking their dogs. Sun sparkled off the waves. I inhaled deeply the fishy smell of ocean, beach, and sand. I sprinted from the whale statue to the great arching mythical bronze sculpture called the Millenniums at the end of the boardwalk. I stopped to read the inscription. *The whole humankind ascends through time in search of peace.* It struck me that peace was the thing Rick had stolen from me long before this final financial explosion. Living with him was an exercise in choosing chaos. Why had I wanted that? I turned around. Sweat trickled down my back. I nodded to an elderly man who strode toward me, pumping his arms energetically through the air. His wife jogged slowly by his side. They greeted me with bony smiles. With Rick, I had been too busy reacting to feel. After Antonio, that had seemed like a good idea. Now it looked to have been a foolish waste of time.

I slowed as I passed a bandstand in the square in front of a church. The cathedral loomed over me, a red brick building with a round tower topped with the type of crown Our Lady of Guadalupe wore in paintings all over town. Rows of concrete steps separated the sanctuary from the street. A sign in the open doorway reminded visitors, in English and Spanish, to respect those worshipping inside. On a whim, I loped up the steps and peered into the darkened interior. The scent of incense filled the air, and all around candles flickered. A huge gold-and-white altarpiece dominated the front. A handful of people knelt in pews, perhaps waiting for morning Mass. Near the front I saw a familiar back, the same one I'd followed around the cliff edge only hours before. I retreated down the church steps and made my way toward work, wondering what it would mean if John didn't call.

***

For the next few days, I jumped every time a phone rang, my heart sinking when I realized it wasn't mine. On Wednesday afternoon, I got a text from a number I didn't know.

Are you free to meet on our beach tonight? 9?

I stared at the screen and smiled. Hell yes.

***

After the dinner service was out, I ran home to shower. Getting ready took longer than I expected, and even though I trotted the last blocks to the cliff, I was a few minutes late. When I rounded the point, I made out a dark figure sitting on the beach. He unfolded as I approached. The moon came out from behind a cloud. He smiled as he walked into the surf toward me. He stretched out his arms, and I was again struck by the image from my dream. I couldn't tell whether he looked like my dream man or I was changing my memory to make John into my merman. Either way, it was crazy how fast my heart was beating.

I splashed the last few steps until I stood looking up into his eyes. "Are your eyes green? I've never seen you in the light." As soon as I spoke, I panicked. Maybe I'd broken the spell.

Instead he cupped my chin and tipped it up. "Sort of hazel. My mother was Irish." I shivered. A deep voice always does it for me, and his floated over me like honey.

A wave crashed into my calves and retreated, sucking sand from beneath my feet. I followed him up the beach to where he'd spread a cotton Mexican blanket. I cleared my throat. "You know, I don't know your last name."

"Giovanni." He took my hand and started to sit. "John Giovanni. Sounds redundant, doesn't it?"

"I'm David Schwartz." I put my hand on his arm. "Can we take our clothes off this time?"

A short laugh burst from him, but he straightened, pulled off his tee, dropped his pants, and stood naked and beautiful in the moonlight. I struggled out of my own clothes.

His skin against mine felt like a miracle. His muscles were like long, lean ropes. I kissed his chest, licked the salt from his skin. He exhaled softly, and we crumpled together onto the blanket.

The sand under the blanket conformed to my shape as I wrapped myself around him. He ran his hand over my head and whispered, "So smooth."

I tongued his jawline. "Smooth, that's me."

"Are you? If there's one thing you could say about me, it's that I'm not smooth at all." He tilted his head, exposing his long neck to my tongue. His cock poked my belly. He opened his thighs and let my cock slip between. When he pressed his thighs closed again, I felt enveloped in his warmth.

"Whatever you are, you feel good to me." I rolled on top of him, enthralled by the feel of the coarse hairs on his thighs and balls rubbing against my cock.

"Good." He kissed me and thrust his tongue deep into my mouth. He tasted like toothpaste. I ran my hand along his smooth, shaven jaw and into the tangle of his hair. I thrust into the clench of his thighs, rubbing my cock along his balls and undulating to stroke his dick with my belly.

His name was John Giovanni. It sounded like a poem. His fingers dug into my ass cheeks, pulling me toward him with every thrust as we rocked together. With each ragged breath, I inhaled his name, like a gift that I gave back with a shout as I crested, spilling against his thighs. A moment later, I felt the warm gush of his response.

I thought if I stayed where I was, I could pin him to the beach for a little longer. But he rolled from under me and sat staring out at the sea. I watched his shoulders rise and fall with his breath.

He turned to look down at me. "You're going back to the States soon, aren't you?"

I hesitated, part of me wanting to tell him I was staying. But I had unfinished business back home. A bankruptcy hearing scheduled for next month. I heard myself say flatly, "Yeah."

John nodded and reached for his clothes. We both started at the sound of women's laughter on the cliff above us.

He jumped up. "Hurry. There's a path down to this beach from the house above. If we don't get out of here, it sounds like we'll have company soon."

I scrambled into my clothes. John pulled on his pants and grabbed his shirt and the blanket. We splashed into the surf and ducked around the boulder, emerging onto the city beach to find a group of young men lounging at the water's edge, sipping from martini glasses.

There were hoots and whistles at the sight of us, half-dressed and drenched from running through the surf. As my feet hit dry sand, I paused to give them a deep bow. They applauded wildly. When I looked up again, John was gone.

Chapter Seven

The manager of the beach hotel was a short man with a pronounced belly. He dressed in black suits, starched, white shirts and skinny ties, and occasionally hovered near the buffet, chatting with the cast and crew members who were also hotel guests. One morning he caught me as I was checking on the canapés.

He gave me a friendly smile. "Your *español* is excellent, almost like you were born here."

I looked up. "*Gracias.* You're kind."

"You like it here in Puerto Vallarta?" He rocked back on his heels, his hands folded over his belly like Humpty Dumpty.

I glanced down the sun-saturated beach. "Of course. It's beautiful."

He looked me over like I was a cake he was considering for his daughter's birthday party. "What will you do after all this"—his hand fluttered toward a cluster of movie people—"is over?"

I shrugged. "I'm not sure yet. Maybe I'll go to LA."

He nodded, his left hand tapping the right. "Maybe you'll decide to stay. If you do, come see me, yes?"

I smiled. "Thank you."

He asked, "You know how to mix drinks?"

My face must have reflected my shock. "I'm a chef, not a bartender."

He waved his hand dismissively. "It is the same thing. You follow a recipe and make something good for the customer. I have cooks. But a handsome American at the bar, that would be good. You'd bring in both boys and girls, yes?"

I tried to hold my face neutral as I gave him a quick bow in appreciation of the offer. I wasn't exactly in a position to dismiss any possible future employment. But mixing drinks? That sounded like a very bad idea. I nodded my thanks and headed toward the trailer.

***

It was midafternoon, and food production lulled. Two women gossiped as they chopped vegetables for a pasta primavera. A teenage boy washed lettuce; another washed dishes. The dinner prep shift wasn't due for an hour. I hung up my chef's coat, stripped off my tee, and stepped outside. I left my shoes at the edge of the boardwalk and curled my toes in the hot sand. To the north, the movie people had cordoned off a section of beach. I could see the director gesticulating to a clump of actors. From a distance, the crash of waves drowned his words. I walked down the beach, stopping as a wave crashed against my shin, the cold water refreshing after the hot sand.

"Too hot in the kitchen?" The deep voice was close behind me, as familiar as my television set, back when I had a television set.

I turned to see the movie star standing out of range of the waves. His chiseled jaw, the dimple, that dirty blond, windswept hair. It was surreal to see him in person, like I'd stepped through the screen. His smile curved up on one side. His gaze stroked down my chest. It would have been sexy if I hadn't known his reputation for fucking anything that stood to pee.

I felt sand slip from beneath my heels as a wave receded.

"You're Kenny's friend, aren't you?" A broad-brimmed visor kept the sun off his face. Sweat beaded on his powdered forehead. His white cotton robe fell to his knees, below which his tanned calves looked as muscular in person as on the big screen.

"I went to cooking school with George."

He tilted his head to the side, a seduction move I'd seen in a dozen of his movies. "I'm not due back on set for another hour, and my suite is air-conditioned."

A wave startled me, splashing all the way to my knee. I took a step up the beach.

I shook my head. "That's a nice offer, but I'm afraid I can't take you up on it."

He raised elegant eyebrows. "You keep turning me down. Is it a boyfriend problem? No one needs to know."

I shrugged. "Thank you anyway. I'm truly flattered."

"He's a lucky boy. Let me know if you change your mind." He contemplated me for a few beats before turning to stroll up the beach and disappearing into the hotel.

I walked back to the boardwalk and retrieved my shoes. Back at the trailer, I found George studying a dry goods cabinet and making notes. I relayed my conversation with the movie star.

George looked at me, pen poised above his clipboard. "So why not take him up on it? He's hot, and you're single."

I wrinkled my nose. "I'm not really interested in casual sex with strangers."

His eyebrows rose. "And what would you call your rendezvous with the merman?"

I shrugged. "Doesn't feel like the same thing at all."

"Interesting." He went back to counting milk bottles. "Happens all the time at home. If it wasn't for Kenny, I'd consider the propositions a job perk."

The trailer was cool compared to the heat outside. I wondered what it would be like to take George up on his employment offer. The whole Los Angeles scene wasn't exactly my style. Neither was delivering production food to dieting masses. On the other hand, my prospects were limited. Puerto Vallarta might be gorgeous, but bartending sounded like a deadly occupation for me. I felt a moment of unexpected compassion for Rick's slip back into gambling. For a drunk like me, when life gave me lemons, it always put me in the mood for vodka with a twist. Clearly my attitude needed some adjustment. I stepped outside to call Ty.

***

When I checked my e-mail after work, there was a note from my bankruptcy attorney. Abe said I had to be back in Portland for something called a meeting of creditors at the end of January. One cousin sent an inspirational chain letter, and another sent a link to a letter to the editor mourning the death of my restaurant. The author called it "Portland's coolest tiny hot spot" and postulated that it had "succumbed to the cancer of soulless corporations spreading through the food industry." I snorted. Cancer, my ass. The poor thing was murdered. I sent Papa a short blast, letting him know I was okay, still sober. There was another e-mail from Rick. I deleted it unopened.

The teenager manning the desk was playing a war game. I interrupted him to let him know I was finished, and walked out into the night. From somewhere down the block, a bass beat boomed. Horns blared. A truck downshifted. A woman with a basket full of fresh tamales called to me. I paid her fifty cents' worth of pesos, and she handed me dinner. The night felt warm and alive. I walked to the Malecon and sat on a bench, watching moonlight sparkling on the sea.

I opened my cell and scrolled through the numbers. Ty, George, Kenny, the tortilla ladies, fish, meat, fruit vendors. And John. I stared at his number. What did it say about me that the best thing I had going in my life was a man with whom I'd exchanged a dozen words and some body fluids? I slapped the phone shut and walked back to my hotel.

I woke early on Friday and slid on my running shoes. With only a few cars on the road, the city was as quiet as it gets. I pounded through the dark, along the uneven pavement, past closed shops and empty food stalls. A memory came to me from my first time in Mexico, early in my stay, before everything blurred to blackout. I'd taken a bus though the streets of Mexico City. It was the middle of the afternoon, and all the seats were taken. I hung on to the cracked vinyl strap in the swaying bus, listening in on conversations and feeling my heart expand. I'd wanted to embrace everyone, swallow the culture whole.

I jogged past the bronze sculpture of a boy riding a seahorse that Puerto Vallarta had taken as its personal symbol, and wondered if that hunger to feel a part of Mexico had died with Antonio or whether I'd feel it again if I stayed long enough.

Chapter Eight

The final weekend shoot was scheduled at an island estate with limited kitchen facilities. The plan was for George to take a skeletal crew and a lot of premade food. Those of us who were to be left behind worked all night Friday. We drank gallons of coffee, told funny stories, complained about our lives, spouses, and children, and diced, sautéed, braised, baked, boiled, and tossed. Toward dawn, a crew of men carted five-gallon buckets full of salads, soups, beans, and batter, boxes of tortillas, baked goods, and canapés to the beach, where sun-scorched men trotted them out to awning-covered boats that whisked them away. I stumbled out of the trailer at sunrise, leaving two sleepy teenagers in charge of cleanup.

The hotel lobby was still dark when I entered. I smiled at the tired-looking clerk and trudged upstairs. I kicked off my shoes and fell into bed. I was asleep before the cathedral bells rang for early Mass. I woke in late afternoon to a hot room and the sounds of traffic, music, and life in the street below. I stared at the ceiling, the afterimages of a dream floating through my mind. This time I could see his face, could see John smiling, his eyes as warm and green as the ocean. For the next twenty-four hours, there was nowhere I needed to be, not until it was time to prep dinner for the wayfaring cast and crew the next day.

I was hungry. And hard. And alone. I spit on my hand, closed my eyes, and imagined myself back on the beach with John.

Later I took a shower, dressed, and went in search of food. I bought three tamales and walked down to the Malecon to people watch. A small army of sand castle artists worked on giant sculptures as tourists took pictures and dropped coins in boxes bolted into the sidewalk. Small children played in the surf. Middle-aged tourists in bathing trunks or sundresses and sandals strolled along eating ice cream and drinking sweaty bottles of beer. Vendors wove between them, hawking jewelry and food and souvenirs. Two men sat on a bench together, watching the sea. Their thighs touched, their heads inclined toward each other, and their lips moved in whispered conversation. I fingered my phone.

Near the center of the Malecon was a circle of bronze sculptures of fanciful sea creatures fashioned into chairs and benches. I sat in the lap of an elongated octopus and flipped open my phone. I stared at his number a long time, wondering what it was about him that made me so reluctant to call. Maybe because he seemed to spook easily.

I took a deep breath and punched Send.

As it rang in my ear, I watched the seagulls picking at trash on the beach and listened to the waves. I was almost ready to give up when I heard him say "hello" in that deep voice that sent shivers all the way down to my groin.

"Hey, it's David." I cleared my throat in the ensuing silence. "From the beach?"

"I know." Was that a good thing or a bad thing? It was impossible to tell from his tone.

"I was wondering if you're free, if you want to hang out." If there was an age where this kind of conversation quit making one feel like an awkward teenager, I hadn't hit it.

"When?" I heard voices in the background on his end.

"Now? Tonight, I mean?"

The voices diminished, like he was walking away from them. "I can't."

"Oh."

His voice rose as he spoke quickly. "I'd like to, really, but—"

Something clicked in my head. Voices, female voices. "Oh, Christ, you're not married, are you?"

"What?" It burst from him with a short laugh. "No. Nothing like that. It's just that I... What time is it?"

I checked my watch. "About four."

"Let me see what I can do. I'll call you soon." The phone went dead.

I stared at it. Soon. Like a few minutes soon or days soon? I shoved the phone in my pocket and stood. Might as well walk toward the pavilion. Maybe I could catch a native dance performance.

My pocket buzzed before I was halfway there.

"David?" He sounded out of breath. "There's a coffee shop on Basilio Badillo. Do you know it?"

"The one with the shelf of English paperbacks?"

"That's it. Meet me there in something over an hour, okay?"

As I rung off, my heart was pounding. My merman and I had a coffee date.

It took less than twenty minutes to walk to the coffee shop. It felt self-indulgent and touristy to order a latte and sit at a table in the sun, watching the other decadent tourists pass by. I tried not to be nervous but found myself shredding my napkin into tiny pieces. I stuffed them in my pocket to keep the bits from blowing away.

John wore loose cotton shorts, and his T-shirt matched his gray-green eyes. He looked focused and sexy as he strode up the street, his dark curls blowing in the wind. I'd been afraid I wouldn't recognize him in the daylight, but I didn't need to worry. It was like an electric spark shot through my veins the moment I saw him. He spotted me and smiled. Christ. I was a goner.

I stood as he approached, feeling that same pull to touch that I'd experienced with him from the first night. John held out his hand. I took it, and he pulled me into a hug that left me lonely when he let go. He folded gracefully into the chair beside me. A waiter materialized. John ordered herbal tea in slightly stilted Spanish.

John turned to me. "Hi."

"I can't believe you came." I cupped the mug to keep from reaching for him.

The waiter appeared again. We paused while he set down John's tea. When he left, John busied himself with the tea bag. After a moment, he spoke. "I don't have much practice with this."

"With what?"

He looked up from his cup, his eyes fastening on mine. "This. You and me. Dating, I guess."

I laughed. "This is a pretty safe date. You already know where I want it to end."

His pupils dilated as he held my gaze.

I leaned forward, whispering, "But this time, please don't leave right after."

He jerked back. I cursed myself. Why did I always have to push things? I sat back in my chair, expecting to see him stand and walk away.

Instead he shook his head and gazed down at the table. "I'm sorry. It's a physical reaction. After we…" He glanced at me from under thick lashes. "After I… It's like I have to move, to get away, not from you but from myself. Guilt, I guess."

"What do you have to feel guilty about?" I pictured a lover at home.

He grimaced. "Nothing. Everything. I can't explain it. Can we not talk about this?"

I nodded. "Sure. I shouldn't have asked."

He shook his head. "No, you have every right to ask. But I don't have a good answer."

We sat for a moment, watching the pedestrian traffic.

John cleared his throat. "So, you're with the movie?"

I raised my eyebrows. "Yeah, how'd you know?"

He shrugged. "It's what everyone's talking about. Are you an actor?"

I laughed. "Thanks for that, but no. I'm a cook."

He smiled. "You feed people? What a wonderful profession."

I think I blushed. I was about to ask what he did when he continued, "When does filming end?"

"Monday."

He nodded and stood. "Then we should make the most of our time. Have you seen the Botanical Gardens?"

I shook my head and gulped the last of my latte.

"They're open late tonight for La Posadas. It's a ways away, though. We'll need to take a cab."

I stood. "I have a scooter."

I led him toward the beach where I'd left the scooter parked on a side street. It started right up. John slid on behind me. I closed my eyes for a moment, reveling in the feel of him pressed against me, his arms wrapping my waist. I leaned my head back against his shoulder.

"We'll scare the natives," he breathed into my neck. I could feel him stirring behind me.

I put the scooter in gear and pulled out.

With gestures and shouted directions, he led me through town and out into forested suburbs. We climbed a hill and turned into a gravel driveway. The parking lot was almost full. I pulled the scooter into an empty spot near the back. John hopped off, shaking out his long legs. A kid came toward the scooter, and John thrust a bill into his hand.

I started for my wallet, but he shook his head. "It's on me." He nodded toward a building at the end of the drive. "Come on. We can look at the orchids before everything begins."

We walked up a long gravel path toward a two-story building surrounded by blooms. The air was thick with the scent of flowers. Ornate, white columns decorated the building. Pink and white flowers cascaded from pots hung in the branches of palm trees. White flowering bushes interspersed with succulents and potted plants bordered the pathway. Small clusters of people chatted together around the building entrance.

"This place is amazing," I whispered.

"Isn't it? Let's go in here." He led me into a greenhouse filled with potted greenery. I moved to examine a spidery orchid.

A voice boomed behind us. "Father John Giovanni. Come to bless the nativities?"

I turned to see John, his lips in a tight smile, shaking the hand of a portly American in a Hawaiian-print shirt. "Not exactly, Frank."

Frank looked around the greenhouse. "Where's Paul?"

John dropped his hand and gestured toward me. "I'm here with my friend, David. This is Frank Wannaker. You may have seen his curio store downtown."

Frank gave me the once-over as he shook my hand. "The Golden Seahorse. Come on in. I'll make you a hell of a deal." He drawled out the last word with a wink.

I was still wondering about the first part of their conversation. Father John? Frank left with a pat on the back for John and another wink for me.

John leaned against a wooden bench and sighed. "Sorry about that. He's a nice man but can be somewhat overbearing."

I was still mulling over the whole "Father" thing but decided to start with the easy question. "Who's Paul?"

"Someone I used to know." He grimaced. "I guess you could call him my ex."

The air in the greenhouse was wet and hot.

John reached out and brushed my arm. "Let's not think about him, okay?"

I nodded. I had an ex I didn't want to think about, too. A gong rang outside. I looked out the windows at people moving toward the building's main entrance. "What's La Posadas?"

John smiled. "It's a traditional Christmas event where we sing carols and parade from one nativity scene to the next."

"Oh. Are Jews allowed?"

"Of course. You're Jewish?"

"With a name like David Schwartz and a nose like this, you could doubt it?"

He ran one long, thin finger down my nose. "I hadn't thought about it. Will it offend you to sing carols?"

"Offend me?" I shook my head. "But I might not know the words."

Outside, dusk darkened the garden. Locals and tourists milled around the courtyard. Frank waved at us from across the way.

I looked at Frank and back at John. "Why did he call you Father?"

John took two lit candles from a tray being passed around by a young Mexican boy. He handed one to me. "I used to be a priest."

I took the candle, still staring at John. "A *priest* priest? I mean like the real thing with celibacy and black robes and incense and chanting and…." I stopped myself before adding anything about altar boys.

He grimaced. "I'm afraid so."

I was still reeling from that when the music began, a Spanish Christmas carol sung in the jagged-voiced chorus of strangers singing together for the first time. The group shuffled forward. A line of bobbing lights developed as people funneled onto a path down the hill.

"Don't freak out, please," John whispered as we walked down the path. We stopped before a poinsettia plant, below which sat a funky homemade Jesus, Mary, and Joseph surrounded by squat, barnyard animals. The group huddled around the manger scene and found an uneven harmony. In the candlelight, the rough clay figures took on an unexpected dignity. The song ended, and the crowd moved again.

I stared at the nativity scene, trying to wrap my mind around the idea of fucking a priest.

John stood beside me, his long arms dangling by his sides. He frowned. "I'm sure you made a few choices you later regretted."

"Yeah." I brushed his fingers with my own. "More than most. Sorry, it was a shock. I'm okay. Let's go see the next Baby Jesus."

John squeezed my hand. "I need to be in Boca early in the morning. Can you drive me?"

I brought his hand to my mouth and kissed his palm. "Will you stay with me until then?"

He shuddered. With one long breath, he blew out our candles. His hand slid out of mine to cradle the back of my neck. His mouth, when it met mine, was his answer.

The night was warm, the music lovely as we walked along the perfumed path, each brush of our hands or arms a tingling promise of the night ahead. I couldn't reconcile the images I had of priests with the sexy man beside me. But my experience of priests was limited to movies and TV: Spencer Tracy in *Boys Town*, Father Guido Sarducci from *Saturday Night Live*, Father Brennan in the *Omen*, and Priest Maxi on *South Park*—a mixed bunch that couldn't possibly represent real people.

We didn't relight our candles and trailed behind the group. After a few minutes the people ahead of us stopped and turned toward the side of the path where another manger scene appeared. Candlelight lit a few faces. As we approached, the singing seemed to swell. John's hand was firm and warm in mine. His voice was deep and clear as he joined in the chorus. I inhaled the thick floral scent coming from a bushy plant nearby. The past, mine and his, seemed to dissolve into one beautiful moment marked by flickering candles and three-part harmony.

The next song hit me like a slap, and I must have flinched.

"What is it?" John's arm slid around me, holding me still as the group moved forward.

I shook my head. "I'm sorry. It's nothing. Just a memory. Someone I knew used to sing that song in the shower."

"Tell me."

I gazed up into the sky. A full moon was rising. Rule number one of first dates—don't talk about ex-lovers. Especially if they're dead. When I focused on John again, I could barely make out his features in the darkness. It occurred to me that as a priest he'd had a lot of practice listening to other people's sorrows.

He took both my hands in his and waited.

It wasn't a story I told people. It wasn't even one I told myself.

"When I was young, I came to study in Mexico and fell in love with a young man. Antonio. He was a true romantic and one of the kindest people I've ever met." I focused on John. He squeezed my hands and nodded for me to continue. I took a deep breath. "He died."

"How?" John's voice was a low whisper.

"In a car wreck. I'd—" I paused, making sure I had my voice under control. "I'd asked him to hurry home after work. He hurried, but he didn't make it home."

John didn't laugh at my lame joke but enfolded me in his arms and pulled me close. We stood in silence, listening to the fading sound of Antonio's favorite carol.

I pulled away and brushed at my eyes.

John rested his hand on my shoulder. "I'm very sorry for your loss. Thank you for telling me."

I nodded and looked way.

He rested his hand on my shoulder. "Do you want to stay for the bonfire, or shall we go now?"

I took his hand and started back up the path, the landscape silver in the moonlight. I felt raw and open—more vulnerable than I had in a long time.

Chapter Nine

The ache of loss that Antonio's memory had opened in me left me craving physical comfort. With John pressed into my back and the scooter motor vibrating my balls, it was amazing we made it back to the hotel room without crashing. The earnest young student from the local university who manned the desk all night raised a tired hand in greeting, barely acknowledging my guest. John followed me, both of us bounding up the stairs in an unseemly hurry. His breath on my neck as I fumbled with my keys sent shivers all the way through me.

When I got the door open, I pulled him in and slammed it closed behind us. John's hands cupped my face as his mouth met mine in an openmouthed, tongue-filled kiss. He tasted like he smelled, spicy with a hint of sea salt on his skin. I slid my hands beneath his tee, running them up his sides. His skin, smooth over taut muscles, felt delicious beneath my fingers. He groaned and pressed his hips to mine. I felt the hard ridge of him against me.

I pulled away. "I want you. And I don't want you to run away. Can that happen?"

His gaze searched mine. "I don't know."

I kissed his neck. He tilted his head, opening up to me. I whispered, "You feel guilty? Like this is wrong? Am I wrestling God for you?"

He laughed. "Like your ancestor Jacob? No, I don't think so."

I ran my thumbs over his nipples, and he shuddered. "Was it the same with Paul? Did you feel guilty then?"

"No." He caressed my shoulders. "It was different. I loved him and believed he loved me."

It's not like I thought we were in love or anything, but I-liked-the-last-guy-better-than-you is always a buzzkill. I stepped away.

John closed his eyes and shook his head. "I'm sorry. That came out badly. I told you, I'm not good at this."

I took a deep breath, grasped his hand, and led him to the bed. I was being ridiculous. Of course this wasn't the same as a long-term relationship. I pulled him to sit beside me. "It's okay."

He turned sideways on the bed to face me and took my hand in both of his. "No. It's not. You deserve better. You're the first man I've been with since Paul." He laughed drily. "Truth be told, you're the second person I've kissed."

"Really?" I guess I shouldn't have been surprised. After all, he'd been a priest. But still, didn't everyone fool around in high school?

He shrugged. "I was young when I felt called to the priesthood. I thought I wouldn't miss what I never tried."

I brushed my lips across his. "And now?"

Amusement played in the creases around his eyes. "I have a lot of time to make up for." His kiss was long and sweet. I let myself fall into the heat of it.

He pulled away, his face serious. He ran his hand over my scalp and let it rest on the back of my neck. "I hear what you're telling me, that it bothers you when I don't stay and cuddle after we… Afterward. I'll try. But if I can't, it's not because of anything about you."

I studied his face, noticed the strong arch of his eyebrows and the dash of gray at his temples. I couldn't imagine spending years celibate within an institution that thought there was sin in something as central to my existence as my sexuality. "They're wrong, you know, about homosexuality. We were born this way."

He shook his head. "It's not that. I came to terms with that a long time ago. It's about what we are to each other. Obviously I think you're special. But David, you're leaving. Which means what happens between us can't be serious. And for me, that feels wrong. And yet I want you so badly that"— his gaze dropped to our hands—"each time I tell myself not to seek you out, that sex without love, without commitment, is…" His eyes met mine again. "But I come to you anyway. I can't stop myself."

Okay. That was hot.

I pulled him to me. He fell into the kiss like a drowning man. I slid his tee up his body, breaking the kiss so I could pull it over his head. He mimicked my movements, his hands hot against my skin as he pulled off my shirt. He trembled. The smell of his sweat, the taste of his mouth, the feel of his stubble scraping my cheek pumped blood from my brain to my cock. His hands fumbled at my buckle. I caressed his arms, trying to calm his trembling. That seemed to make it worse.

I broke our kiss long enough to slide out of my pants and help him out of his. Cool fluorescent light fell from the overhead fixture. I took in the lean contours of his muscles, his tan lines, the dark curl of his pubic hair, the straight, strong line of his cock. "You're fucking gorgeous." Could I say *fuck* around a priest? I supposed that if we could do it, I could say it.

He looked down at himself. "You think so? Thank you." When he looked up, his eyes crinkled with amusement again. "You probably say that to all the boys."

I snorted. "Right. I'm slamming them left and right."

His brow wrinkled. "Aren't you? I assumed since we met at the bar and—"

I ran a finger through the dark cluster of hairs on his chest, letting my finger trail over to circle around his nipple. "Nope. You're the first new partner I've had in years." I wrapped my legs around him so we were sitting within the cradle of each other's legs, our cocks barely brushing. He leaned to kiss me, but I held him away, one hand in the center of his chest. "Maybe it would help if we got to know each other."

"Are you testing my self-restraint?" He caressed my jaw with his thumb.

I laughed and leaned into his touch. "More like drawing out the time I have with you. I promise, you'll get what you want in the end."

His eyes had a warm, sexy sadness to them. I saw gold flecks embedded in the green. "Will I?"

I leaned in to kiss him, slipping my tongue into his mouth as I thumbed his nipples. He groaned, burying his hands in my hair. I felt the swell of his cock against mine.

"Fuck it. I'll get to know you later," I whispered into his mouth, hauling him down on top of me.

He cradled my face, pressing his tongue deep into my mouth. I stroked the long muscles of his back. His skin felt soft, like a rose petal I'd picked up from the path at the gardens. A horn honked on the street outside. A rap song throbbed from far away. The cathedral bell chimed, striking the hour. John tensed. He surged against me, thrusting fiercely.

I threw out a hand and fumbled open the bedside table drawer, feeling around until I found one of the foil packets and lube pillows I'd stashed in there in a hopeful moment. Holding up the condom, I said, "If I wake up alone in the morning, I want to feel that you've been here."

Color drained from his face as he looked at the red-and-white foil package. He swallowed. "I've never—"

"Really?" I blinked at him. He had to be what, forty? Right, he'd been a priest.

He took a deep breath. "It's not something Paul ever—"

I twirled the condom between my fingers and caressed his ass with my ankle. "You want to give it a try?"

He looked into my eyes. Whatever he saw there made his face soften. He brushed his hand across my cheek. "I don't want to hurt you."

I ripped open the package and pulled out the slick rolled disk. "A little pain never hurt anyone." At his panicked look, I added, "Don't worry. You won't do permanent damage. And who knows, you might like it. I know I will." I rolled the lubricated condom onto his cock, broke open the lube pillow, and greased him up. John held himself up with his arms while I squirmed underneath him to position my asshole against the tip of his cock.

When was the last time I'd slept with a virgin? High school? "You okay?"

He nodded. "Are you sure you want this?"

Was I sure? My ass pulsed with need for him. If he didn't fuck me soon, I thought I'd explode. I looked up into his eyes. "Yes. Please."

He hesitated. I held his gaze. His eyes darkened. Something flickered across his face, the hint of smile, a shadow of warmth. I pulled my knees to my chest, exposing myself to him. His eyes never left mine as he pushed. It had been a long time. My ass clenched with the burn. John stopped, his brow creasing. I took a deep breath and let it out, willing myself to relax. I nodded, and he slid in more. I shifted until he hit the spot, and the burn turned into a fire.

"Oh yeah," I whispered, and something unlocked in John. He plunged into me. I drove back toward him. Sweat beaded my skin. Traffic sounds outside faded, replaced by the grunt and gasp of our breaths, as my whole world shrunk to the feel of John's cock thrusting into me. His mouth fell open. His curls lay flat, plastered to his forehead. I could see his pulse beating in his throat, and still his gaze held mine. The intensity with which he looked at me felt even more intimate than his cock buried deep in my ass. It was like he was trying to climb inside both my body and soul. I felt consumed by the hunger in his eyes and the force of his cock pounding into me. I didn't want it to end. I refused to touch myself, as if by holding my orgasm back I could hold him, could keep us joined cock-to-ass forever in a driving free fall of skin and heat and heart, and it kept coming anyway, cresting over me at the instant I saw it hit John, and I was coming and coming, spurting wildly onto his belly, my hands digging into his back as I felt the pulse of him in my ass.

He collapsed onto me, and I clutched him, determined to hold on for as long as I could.

"David," he whispered as his breath slowed.

"I know." I let him go, wincing as he pulled out of me. He lay on his side, his head cradled in his hand. I could see the deliberate rise and fall of his chest like he was trying to breathe through whatever it was that made him run away.

He gazed at the merman hanging on my wall for a long moment before glancing down at me. "Paul argued that sodomy was the sin. He thought that as long as we refrained from that, we'd be safe."

I shook my head. "And were you also avoiding the other abominations listed in Leviticus, like eating shrimp and wearing cotton-linen blends?"

He smiled sadly. "Apparently I'm not avoiding any of them." He sat up. "I'm sorry, but I need to go for a walk or something. I'll be back."

"For what it's worth, I doubt God cares what we do in bed." I gestured toward the key where it sat on the bedside table. "Take that with you."

He ran a hand across my brow. "I'm sure God cares a great deal, but perhaps more about how we treat each other than what exactly we do in bed and with whom." He stood abruptly, pulled on his shorts, grabbed my key, and left, shutting the door quietly behind him. I listened to the slap of his bare feet on the steps until I couldn't hear them anymore and lay in the dark thinking about abominations.

As a child I went to Hebrew and Sunday school at a Reform Jewish temple where the six hundred and thirteen Biblical Laws were taught as choices, many of which were nothing more than quaint strictures of historical interest. It wasn't easy for my parents when I came out, but at least we'd all been spared the belief in a punishing God. Evidently it wasn't that simple for John. Or maybe he was telling the truth, and being queer didn't have anything to do with his guilt.

Feeling bad about sex without love was something I equated with my parents' generation and abandoned pregnant women, not with real life in the twenty-first century.

I must have dozed off, because the next thing I knew, he was shaking my shoulder, whispering, "David, wake up. I need you to drive me to Boca."

***

The streets felt surreal and empty in the early dawn. The light grew, sparkling off the ocean as we rode down the coastal highway to Boca de Tomatlan, the small town bordering Puerto Vallarta to the south. With the wind in my face and John pressed against my back, it could have felt impossibly romantic. Except I was leaving in a week, and between my nonstop work and John's cryptic life, I doubted we'd see each other again.

I ignored the ache in my chest as we rolled down the steep slope to Boca Bay. John pointed toward the beach where a squat Mexican man stood holding a battered fishing boat by a thin rope. The boat bounced against the shore behind him like a pet on a leash. I stopped at the edge of the pavement, and John slipped off. I shivered from the sudden touch of cool air on my back.

John stood beside the scooter, his hands stuffed into his pockets.

I held his gaze for as long as I could.

He puffed out air from between his lips. "Good luck with the rest of your movie."

"Thanks."

He grimaced. "What's the etiquette for this? I don't know what to say."

I shrugged. "Not much to say. If you're ever in Portland…"

The man on the beach called to him. John started. "I have to go."

"I know."

He started down the beach. After a few steps he turned back. "Last night was…"

"Yeah, for me too."

He took a step toward me and stopped. "I wish we had more time."

I nodded.

He reached out and touched my cheek before turning to sprint down the beach. I watched him splash into the water and fling himself into the boat as the other man pushed it away from shore.

John lifted his hand. I waved in return. I watched until I heard the boat motor start, turned my scooter around, and started back up the hill. I thought about Portland and all that waited for me there. What I wanted was to race back down the hill, jump onto John's boat, and escape everything. But I had already tried that the years I spent swimming in a bottle of tequila. Acting like a grown-up can sometimes break your heart.

Chapter Ten

I drove home through the brightening streets. Puerto Vallarta woke up around me. Where on the way out we'd encountered only delivery trucks and buses, going home I had to weave around cars and carts and every imaginable form of transportation. The drive back took twice as long as the drive out, and without the press of John against my back, the wind was cold. My eyelids drooped.

The desk clerk had coffee on by the time I got back. I grabbed a cup and a handful of cardboard cookies and trudged up the three flights to my room. Opening the door, I was hit by a visceral sense of John. There was the smell of sex and the lingering scent of his skin. It struck me, as I stared at the rumpled sheets, that John must be even more tired than I was, since he hadn't slept all night. Maybe it was my romantic side, or possibly some sort of competition with the phantom Paul, but I suddenly wanted to know what it felt like to sleep all night next to John, to wake up to sex in the predawn gray. The thought that I might leave Mexico without seeing him again was impossibly sad.

I looked at my watch. I didn't need to be at work for hours. Wherever John was going so early in the morning, it didn't mean he'd be there all day and all night. It wouldn't hurt to ask.

I thumbed through the numbers on my phone until I got to John's and sent him a quick text. I heard the distinctive sound of a cell phone vibrating against a hard surface and looked up to see John's phone sitting on the windowsill next to the empty Hanukkah menorah. I gazed at it for a long moment. He'd left his phone. I smiled. Now I had an excellent excuse to contact him again. All I had to do was figure out how to get it to him. I picked up his phone and glanced at my text on the display. I opened his contacts list, thinking I could use it to find out where he was, maybe call someone, and ask. Except there was only one contact listed. Me.

I sat down on the bed and eyed the phone, registering that it was very like my own, a cheap model with prepaid minutes, useful for tourists, temporary workers, criminals, and someone having an affair. I tried to think of some other reason John would have this kind of phone. Nothing came to mind. I remembered the guy from the garden, Frank, asking about Paul. Maybe John had exaggerated that breakup. No, that didn't feel right. Did priests lie? Ex-priests. The choirboy abuse scandals came to mind. Evidently priests did a lot of things you wouldn't expect.

"I guess you could call him my ex." That's what John had said. And he hadn't freaked out when Frank saw us together. So what did that mean? I rubbed the bridge of my nose. The whole thing was giving me a headache. I flopped back on the

bed, closed my eyes, tried to ignore the scent of him on the sheets, and fell asleep.

When I woke, it was noon, and the room was hot. My little room looked shabby and unkempt in the bright afternoon light. I saw it through a stranger's eyes—the backpack leaning against one wall, clean clothes in sloppy piles on the desk, dirty ones heaped in the corner. Dust covered the windowsill where the Hanukkah menorah still sat, crusty drippings of wax clinging to its sides. I'd hoped to bring him back here, so why hadn't I cleaned up?

I lay in bed, watching dust motes dance in a beam of sunlight, and tried to make sense of everything I knew about John. He was gorgeous. He used to be a priest. That was about it. Much didn't make sense, from his one-number contact list to his push-me-pull-you intimacy dance. Various explanations came to mind—he could be lying about the priesthood. He might be involved or married, a criminal, in the witness protection program, crazy, or simply another damaged soul like me. Given that I was leaving the country in less than a week, it shouldn't have mattered. But I didn't want to return to my emotionally and financially bankrupt life without seeing him one more time.

***

The Golden Seahorse turned out to be a huge antique store/junk shop a few blocks from the waterfront. A lovely Mexican woman stood behind the counter. Another approached me as soon as I entered, asking if she could help.

Before I could say anything, Frank appeared from behind a beaded curtain.

He smiled his recognition. "David, isn't it?"

I shook his hand. "Great shop you have here."

"Thanks." He gave me a slow, appraising look. "Nice of you to stop by. Are you in the market for souvenirs, or can I interest you in something more personal?"

I sidestepped the question as best I could. "Actually I came to see if you can help me get in touch with John."

He glanced at the clerks, who were openly watching our exchange. Frank motioned for me to follow. "Come on back, and I'll get us a beer."

"Um, thanks, but I don't drink." I pushed through the swinging beads after him.

He looked over his shoulder. "Interesting."

The back room was furnished with a couch, table and chairs, and an old, round-edged refrigerator. A long counter spanned the far wall. Everything was covered with old stuff.

Frank pointed to the couch. "Have a seat, and I'll see what I've got to drink. Sorry about the mess. I scored big at an estate sale last week, and I'm trying to get things priced."

I moved a painted, wooden medicine cabinet to the floor and sat. Frank's head disappeared into the open refrigerator. When he emerged, he held a beer in one hand and a can of soda in the other. He thrust the soda at me and perched on the edge of the table.

He surveyed me as he twisted the cap off his beer. "And why would you be looking for our Johnny?"

I met his gaze. "He left something in my room last night."

Frank chuckled. "At least you're honest. And handsome enough to make me believe you. But why, my dear, didn't he give you a way to get in touch himself?"

I dug in my pocket and brought out John's phone. "I had his number, but he left his phone."

Frank's eyebrows rose. "John has a phone? It's news to me." He held out his hand, and I reluctantly placed the phone in his palm. Frank flipped it open and thumbed the keys.

He looked at me. "There's only one number in the contacts."

I shrugged. "I know. Mine."

Frank put the phone down on the table next to a large, green glass ball and sipped his beer. He stared at the ceiling. I looked around the room. I could only identify half the stuff. It all looked old and worn. Even over the thick scent of furniture polish and soap, I could smell Frank's beer. It made my throat itch in a way I hadn't felt in a long time.

His gaze drifted down to meet mine. "Johnny likes his privacy. He came down here to disappear. I can't tell you where he is, but when I see him next, I'll give him back the phone and tell him you were asking. He can contact you if he wants."

I leaned forward, trying to keep the whine out of my voice. "I leave for the States on Friday. The number in that phone won't work after that."

Frank reached behind him and produced a pad and paper. "Write down your contact information. I'll make sure he gets it with the phone."

I felt him watching me as I scribbled. Frank didn't seem like a particularly trustworthy guy, and nothing in their exchange the night before had given me the impression he and John were best friends, but it was the only thread I had. I handed him the note with my e-mail address and my father's number and address, which was the best I could do for permanence.

Frank examined it. "Portland. You're a long way from home."

"I'm here with the movie crew."

His smile was more of a leer. "I met your movie star the other night at a bar. Nice ass on that one. And a very friendly guy. How'd you meet John?"

I met his gaze. "At a bar."

Frank blinked. "It's true, then, that he and Paul split up."

I shrugged. "I don't know."

Frank knit his eyebrows together and slid down to sit in a chair facing me. "If he really was with you last night, they must have broken up. John isn't the type to play around." He drummed his fingers on his knees. "I'd heard Paul went back up north, but it's hard to believe."

I shifted uncomfortably. I hated the idea of listening to Frank gossip about John, but how the hell else was I going to get the information I wanted? It wasn't like John was exactly forthcoming. I cleared my throat. "How long were they together?"

Frank leaned forward, his voice conspiratorial. "I only know what I heard when they first came down here about four years ago, but the story is that John wanted to get Paul away from the States, from family pressure, the Church, and all the scandal. Didn't know a word of Spanish when they got here. John picked it up pretty quickly, but Paul never seemed to have the heart for it. I guess I'm not surprised he left. But poor John must be heartbroken."

I tried not to grimace. "He was pretty attached?"

Frank looked at me incredulously. "Attached? John left fucking God for Paul. Loved him more than God. If that's not devotion, I don't know what is."

When I stumbled out onto the sidewalk a few minutes later, I wasn't sure if I was glad I'd gone in. *Loved him more than God.* Not exactly how I'd felt about Rick. Or even about Antonio, although I'd mourned him for a long, long time. Perhaps it was a good thing I was headed back north before I got my heart broken by a guy who wasn't over his ex. I checked my watch. If I hurried, I could make a Sunday-afternoon meeting and still be at work on time.

***

The cast and most of the crew flew home on Monday, carrying bags of Mexican gifts to stuff in those fabled stockings hung by the chimney with care. Kenny and George hopped a water taxi for an island getaway. To me, Christmas was about short lines at movie theaters and Chinese takeout, so I volunteered to settle accounts and get the trailer ready to head north.

On Christmas Eve afternoon, the kitchen crew and I piled all the leftover food on the prep tables. I cranked up the music and held a farewell party. I handed out envelopes of pesos and spent an hour saying good-bye. Flush with cash, the crew was a cheerful lot, but the party left me feeling sad. Work was scarce. Those last paychecks would need to stretch a long way. It felt like I was closing my restaurant all over again.

In the evening, I watched the sunset from the Malecon. The restaurants closed early, and traffic was sparse. The next morning the city seemed asleep.

My phone didn't ring. No texts. No e-mails. Nada.

George and Kenny came back the next day, saying they'd decided to stay on through New Year's. They'd heard of a little town down the coast that they wanted to visit. My plane left in the late afternoon. I hugged them good-bye at the hotel. I handed George my phone and scooter keys. He wrote me a check big enough that there might be some left after the bankruptcy court took its cut.

Ty took me to the airport in his battered, brown truck. Over the past few days I'd probably called him too often and babbled too much about my inability to find John. He'd been an incredibly patient friend, and I was truly grateful. He dropped me at the curb with a final, "Take it easy, buddy. And keep in touch."

Late that night, after stumbling through customs, I walked out into the freezing Portland rain. Fucking great to be home.

Chapter Eleven

After a month in Mexico, Portland felt cold to me. On New Year's Eve, Papa and I watched a movie and went to bed early. The next week the rain beat incessantly, and my father's backyard turned into a muddy swamp. I sat at the kitchen table and called every restaurant I knew, people I'd spoken with every year at the Bite of Oregon, whose restaurants I'd visited and who had visited mine. I got a frostier reception than I had the month before. Some were polite, others dismissive, but no one had a job for me. Before I'd left, I had a few who thought there might be something after the holidays. While I was sweating in a tin kitchen, those possibilities had somehow dried up.

In between rejections and organizing my paperwork for bankruptcy, I watched daytime TV. I went to bed early and got up late and was sometimes rewarded with dreams of John. The only good thing in my life was elusive, mysterious, and over two thousand miles away. Time crawled. I felt suspended like a mandarin orange in one of those hideous, retro gelatin desserts. There was nothing I could do but wait for the end of the month and my official insolvency. And after that, my best bet looked like Los Angeles and a job I didn't like, working for someone I did. Or I could keep sitting in the rec room at my father's place, only getting off the couch to make dinner.

***

My court date finally came. Abe had told me to meet him in room 223 of the Gus J. Solomon Courthouse at a quarter to nine. He also assured me it was a formality.

"They do five or six of these things an hour," he'd growled over the phone the night before. "You have to show your face, answer a few questions, and that's it. Your creditors all got notice of the meeting. Don't worry. They never attend."

My best slacks and white cotton shirt had wrinkled in the suitcase, so I'd spent the evening ironing.

Papa offered to give me a ride and keep me company, but I wanted to keep the humiliation to a dull roar. The fewer witnesses, the better. Gray skies, forty degrees, and light rain—a mild winter day in the Pacific Northwest. Quite a shock after sunny Mexico. I shrugged on my raincoat and caught an early bus crowded with people on their way to work. The rain let up, and I got out at Burnside to walk.

People passed me, their work clothes peeking out from under shiny raincoats, their shoes clicking purposefully along the pavement. Everyone on their way to a job except David. I almost stumbled over the mound of dirty blankets covering a cluster of bodies sleeping in a doorway and decided to quit feeling sorry for myself. I might be back at my father's house, but at least it was warm and safe.

Charmaine was working the early shift at one of the carts up on Alder, which is why I'd come down early. I found her leaning out the window of a bright red food truck, serving coffee, and breakfast burritos. She'd sounded wary on the phone, but when she saw me, her smile was broad.

She made a sweeping gesture with her arm. "Hey, boss, come on around back."

The construction worker she was serving glanced at me as I passed, before returning his attention to doctoring his coffee and scooping heaping spoonfuls of salsa onto his burrito.

I climbed the two rickety metal steps into the food truck. It was warm inside, and the smell of cooking tomatoes sent a wave of Mexican nostalgia through me.

"You look good," I told her, and she did. She'd wrapped her hair up in a swath of red-and-black cloth, which matched the beads on her braids, and the steam inside the truck had turned her cheeks a rich mahogany.

She looked me up and down with a slow, assessing gaze. "So do you. Better than I expected."

I laughed. "I didn't have time to get a tan in Mexico, if that's what you mean."

A customer at the window asked for the special. I watched Charmaine pull a flour tortilla from the steam table and fill it with spoonfuls from various metal bins. I noted vaguely the arrangement of the food—hot on the right, cold on the left. Something about her silence had my stomach clenching.

After she'd given the customer his breakfast and his change, Charmaine turned to me. She put her hands on her hips. "Tell me the truth. Are you drinking again?"

I stared at her. The truck felt way too hot. I took a deep breath and shook my head. "No. Why would you think that?"

She nodded. "I didn't think you would. But there's a rumor going around that closing the restaurant sent you into a tailspin."

I squinted at her. "You know where this rumor started?"

She shrugged. "You got me that job working Friday and Saturday at the new place down by the river. People there were asking me about it."

I closed my eyes and leaned up against the door. There are good things and bad things about working in a tightly connected community. This was one of the bad things. I ran down the list of my enemies, trying to figure out who was poisoning my well. I'd defaulted on debts all around town, to local farmers, my landlords, wine vendors, the utilities, my employees—the list was unfortunately long. Except I couldn't think of a reason for any of them to pick that particular, personally devastating form of revenge. And if I thought about it, there was only one bad guy in my life right now. What had I ever seen in him?

I heard Charmaine taking an order at the window, opened my eyes, found the coffee machine and cups, poured a decaf, and passed it to the customer.

Charmaine smiled. "Thanks, boss."

I shrugged. "Probably as close as I'll get to working in this town anytime soon, don't you think?"

"It's not fair. You should fight it."

I dribbled some water from the truck sink onto a dish towel and started wiping the counters for her. "My grandfather used to tell this story from the old country. A rabbi caught one of his congregation gossiping about his neighbor. So he tells the guy to meet him on the roof of the tallest building in town and to bring a feather pillow. The guy doesn't want to piss off the rabbi, so he goes. As soon as he arrives, the rabbi grabs his pillow and rips it open, shaking it out in the wind. Feathers go everywhere, all over town. The guy cries, 'Rabbi, what have you done? How will I get the feathers back into my pillow?' And the rabbi says, 'Ah, now you know. Once a rumor leaves your lips, the wind can take it anywhere. It would be easier to find all your feathers than to take back what you have said about your neighbor.'"

I heard her sigh and had to look away from the compassion in her eyes as she asked, "What will you do?"

I tossed the dishrag back in the sink and glanced around at the tin walls of the trailer. It was smaller than George's, but at least it had a window. Maybe with time I could get used to working inside a box. "I have a friend in LA who runs a catering business. I'll see what he can find me down there."

She gave me a long hug before I left. The air outside felt twice as cold as it had before I stepped into the truck. The rain had started again. Walking toward the courthouse, I watched a guy picking up soggy cigarette butts and storing them in a torn paper cup. It could always get worse.

***

The Gus J. Solomon Courthouse was a beautiful building with art deco bronze lights, filigree doors, marble floors, and a bank of old-fashioned postal boxes along one wall of the ground floor. A sign on one side of the lobby indicated the way to room 223. My footsteps echoed as I crossed the lobby. A woman came out of an office door. She glanced at me in passing, and I felt a wave of humiliation rise from my toes, wondering if she could tell why I was there. I pushed a button, and the door opened on an ancient elevator with bronze walls and worn carpet. Stepping inside, I smelled the dust and imagined I could feel the despair of hundreds, maybe thousands of broken people who had ridden there before me.

The elevator opened onto a long hallway, at the end of which Rick lounged against the wall. I almost punched the elevator button again to close the door against him. Instead I stepped onto the beige-carpeted floor and waited while he sprinted toward me.

I'd forgotten how good he looked. Rick might not have had a soul, but he had a hell of a physique. He smiled at me, and I had a sudden impulse to forgive him everything. I shook it off. I deserved better. I always had.

He was wearing a suit, the blue serge we bought together when he had to go East for his father's fourth wedding. We'd only been together a year, and Rick had been furious that I wasn't invited. I told him not to worry about it, that he looked handsome, have fun, hurry home. I'd dropped to my knees right there in the dressing room, wanting him to think of me every time he wore that suit. The thought of how often I'd been on my knees with him, figuratively and literally, made my stomach clench. I was wearing slacks, a white shirt with tiny food stains on one cuff, and a borrowed tie. I'd sold all my suits, and almost everything else I owned, to cover Rick's debts. After the first time, when he lost our vacation money, why had I believed he'd change?

He stopped a few feet from me. "Hey, Dave. How was Mexico?"

I ground my teeth and stared at him. "What the fuck are you doing here?"

He cleared his throat. "Listen, I know we've had some bad shit between us lately, but I really wanted to be here for you."

I narrowed my eyes and waited.

He fidgeted. "It's my car. I need you to sign a reaffirmation agreement as the cosigner. I swear I'll keep up the payments, but the bank needs a backup. You gotta do this for me. I need my car."

Rick was the kind of guy who walked into a room and had everyone begging for his attention. I looked into those clear blue eyes, as sweet and hot as always. That melting look that held the promise of pornographic pleasures got me every time. Even now, on my way to debase myself over his debts, I felt the erotic pull. Until I reminded myself how much it cost. "Did you tell people I started drinking again?"

"No, of course not. Why would I do that?" But he wouldn't meet my gaze.

I snorted. "Oh, let me see, so I couldn't impugn your sorry-ass credibility by telling the truth about how you gutted our business? No, I will not agree to cosign for your fucking car. I don't have a car anymore, Rick. I let the bank repossess it. Now if you'll excuse me, I'm due in court." I brushed past him and down the hall. He followed me, talking all the way, but I was too busy clenching my jaw and trying not to hit him to listen to anything he said.

I turned a corner and saw Abe. Rick must have seen him too because the noise behind me stopped.

Abe smiled as he held out his hand for me to shake. "You ready? I signed us in. We'll need to sit through a few other hearings, but they don't take long. Let's take a seat inside."

It was quiet inside the room, despite the small clusters of people seated in the audience. Abe and I took our place in a middle row of cushioned blue chairs. At the front of the room was a square wooden table with an ergonomic office chair on one side and uncomfortable wooden ones on the others. On either side were flags—the United States on the right, Oregon on the left. I could feel the fear, my own and everyone else's as the judge or magistrate or whatever she was came into the room and sat in the comfy chair.

Abe patted my hand and whispered, "Relax. It will be okay."

The woman in charge called a name, and a middle-aged couple shuffled forward and sat at the wooden table. I listened as they answered her questions and described the medical expenses—triple bypass surgery with no insurance—that had brought them to this point. For the next man it was a divorce. After that came a woman whose insurance had run out halfway through her cancer treatments. A gambling boyfriend wasn't sounding half as tragic as it had before I came.

For my turn, I disclosed my assets, or lack thereof, and handed over my pay stub from Mexico. When she asked if there were any creditors present, I glanced out at the row of mostly empty chairs. Rick wasn't there.

And it was over.

Out in the hallway, Abe clapped me on the back. "How does it feel to be a free man again?"

I smiled as an unexpected relief flooded through me. Free. What a great concept. "Good. It feels good." Except I didn't have a job, my credit was trashed, and all of Portland thought I was a drunk. But other than that, things were looking up.

Chapter Twelve

Papa tried to press more money on me, but I refused it. As much as I knew he offered in love, at that moment in my life it felt too much like indebtedness. Surprisingly I didn't feel broke. The court had left me three-quarters of the money George paid for my weeks in Mexico. I left a message on George's phone telling him I was on my way to Los Angeles. On an online ride board, I found someone leaving on Saturday who, for a hundred bucks in gas money and a pledge to drive from midnight to four, offered me the one remaining seat in his car.

The night before I left town, I had the dream again. No snakes, no terror, simply the merman walking out of the sea. This time it was clear. He looked and felt and tasted like John. I woke hard and took myself in hand with an ache in my chest.

I made Papa his favorite omelet in the morning as a way of saying thank you. He hugged me hard when he dropped me downtown on his way to work. I waited for my ride under the awning of a coffee cart. When it arrived, the car was a banged-up hatchback and its owner a nineteen-year-old college dropout who looked like he smoked too much dope. There was also a guy in his thirties stinging from a nasty divorce, which he told us all about in the first hour of the drive. The third passenger was a girl, maybe twenty, pretty and small. As soon as she found out I was gay, she latched on to me like I was a life preserver. I didn't blame her. The guys seemed nice enough, but there would be some lonely stretches along the I-5.

The plan was to drive straight through the night and get to Los Angeles sometime midmorning Sunday. I had the midnight-to-four shift. The girl sat up front with me. She was supposed to help me stay awake in the wee hours of the morning but fell asleep around one. I didn't mind. As the radio spewed classic rock, the night opened before me. Speeding through the mountains of Northern California in the middle of the night, officially bankrupt and rumored to be drunk, I had expected to feel depressed. Instead I found myself smiling, the heavy gnaw of worry I'd been living with for months gone.

I was sleeping as the car pulled into a fenced parking lot across from the downtown Los Angeles bus station the next day. We'd agreed on the way down that, what with the bank of phones, and access to transportation, that was the best place to drop the three of us. After rainy Portland it felt good to get out and stretch in the warm, dry air. We shook hands with a half hug, four people who'd spent too much time in a small space. We scattered like the strangers we were. I slung my pack onto my back and walked into the bus station in search of the promised bank of phones.

First I called Papa to let him know we arrived safely.

"A friend of yours from Mexico called last night," he told me after we got through the niceties.

My heartbeat doubled. "Who?"

"Wait, I wrote it down." I heard him shuffling papers. "John Giovanni. I told him you'd left for Los Angeles, and he said to wish you good luck."

"Did he leave a number?"

Something in my voice must have tipped him off. His reply was super gentle. "No, sorry, son. And the caller ID said 'International Call' when I picked it up."

"If he calls back…" I couldn't think of what to have Papa ask John.

My father's voice was low. "I'll have him leave a number so you can call."

"Thanks." I was afraid if I stayed on much longer, my voice would crack. "I'll call you when I'm settled. Don't worry, okay?"

"You're a good man, David. I'm proud of who you are."

After that remark I really was going to cry, so I said good-bye and hung up. I closed my eyes and laid my forehead against the cool metal face of the wall phone. I'd missed him by less than a day. Hours. And now he had disappeared again.

I turned around. The station was crowded. A couple of guys lay sleeping on the floor in one corner. Whether they were homeless or waiting for a bus was hard to tell. All the seats in the waiting area had been taken by a broad spectrum of humanity from a well-dressed black matron, holding her bag over her knees and staring straight ahead, to a drunk frat boy puking into a paper bag. I wondered if young girls from Iowa still rode the bus into Los Angeles hoping to make it in the movies and if this was where they ended up, and whether somewhere in that swarm of weary travelers were predators waiting for them.

I looked at the signboard. There were buses leaving soon for Topeka, Seattle, Phoenix, San Diego, and Tijuana. I stared at that last one for a long time. Here I was with nothing more than the pack on my back and the remnants of my last paycheck, about to beg a friend for a job I didn't want and a place to stay in a town I didn't like. I had my good cooking knives with me, along with my warm-weather clothes.

The money left in my bank account would go a heck of a lot further in Mexico than it would here in the City of Expensive Angels.

I turned back to the phones and dialed George's number. When I told him I'd changed my mind, he sounded disappointed but said he understood. That was good, because I wasn't sure I understood myself. I only knew that if I didn't want to spend the rest of my life wondering what would have happened, then I had to take this chance.

I redialed my papa. "I'm gonna keep going. It'll take me a few days, so you won't hear from me right away, but I don't want you to worry."

He was silent a long time. "Are you sure this is a good idea?"

"No," I admitted. "Not sure at all. But can you do me a favor? If I give you an e-mail address—it's for Ty; he's sort of my sponsor in Mexico—will you send him a note telling him I'm coming down and will be looking for work?" I had no idea if Ty could find work for me, but I knew that saying the magic word *sponsor* to my father would go a long way toward making him feel better. I'd put him, and my mother, through hell the last time I moved to Mexico. The least I could do was keep him from worrying this time. I felt his relief as he agreed. I gave him Ty's address and promised to let him know I was safe as soon as I could.

A surly woman at the counter sold me a ticket for the next Tijuana bus, scheduled to leave in an hour. I bought a couple of bottles of water and a bag of chips at a seedy convenience store and, like the rest of the homeless men, sat on the floor to wait.

Two men in dark suits walked past me, deep in conversation. They both wore white priestly collars. I wondered what it would be like to commit my life to a religious community that viewed my sexuality as inherently sinful. And what would it take to walk away? John said it was the lack of relationship that made him uncomfortable after sex. Was it also self-hatred, pounded into him by years in the Church? Still there must have been compensations, or John wouldn't have become a priest in the first place. Nothing was all bad, not even life with Rick.

The bus was only half an hour late. I checked my pack underneath, and clutching my chips and water, I climbed onto the bus. All the seats near the front were taken, so I shuffled toward the back and found one a few rows from the end. The chemical smell from the toilet wasn't overpowering. Fortunately the guy muttering to himself kept going past me. A teenager with glazed eyes sat beside me, a harsh rap beat audible from his earbuds. I leaned my head against the window and tried to sleep.

***

The bus dropped us off at the border. The mumbling guy, me, the teenager with glazed eyes, a couple of Hispanic women, an elderly couple, and a dozen drunken young men joined a stream of people walking the concrete pathway to Mexico. I caught a glimpse of the ocean through the bars that framed the sidewalk, presumably to keep us contained in a steady stream into Mexico. We filed through a tall, one-way turnstile and were out of the United States. Another few minutes of walking brought us to another turnstile. One at a time we spun through it and spilled out into Mexico. As I walked across the border, no one asked for my paperwork. If my current adventure didn't work out, the line would be longer and slower going back.

I spent a few months in Tijuana all those years ago. I don't remember much, but just knowing I was there made my mouth water, and I could almost taste the tequila. Now, the streets nearest the border were lined with *farmacias*— drugstores where gringos could stock up on all those expensive drugs their insurance wouldn't pay for. I followed the tourists into town. The central bus station, where I could get a camion—a long-haul bus going south—was too far to walk.

One of the few things I remembered from traveling that way back in the day was to load up on supplies before boarding. Back then I'd been content with a few bottles of amber love to keep me going on a long trip. This time I planned to take something more substantial.

I stopped at an ATM and withdrew the equivalent of two hundred dollars. A fruit stand had tiny local oranges. I bought a handful, plus some cheese, nuts, a kilo of tortillas, and two giant bottles of water from a small grocery. An old man in torn jeans was selling brightly colored blankets by the side of the road. I chose one with various shades of green and blue that ranged from the color of the ocean to the exact hue of John's eyes. It can get cold on a camion. I blew a few dollars' worth of pesos on a taxi to the bus station.

There wasn't a direct bus from Tijuana to Puerto Vallarta, but there was one leaving for Tepic right away. It cost half my cash to buy a ticket that would get me most of the way to Puerto Vallarta. I stowed my backpack beneath the bus, and with my blanket draped over my shoulders, my food in a blue plastic bag, I climbed on and found a seat near the front. The bus smelled cleaner than the last one. A Mexican man in his fifties sat next to me. His suit cuffs were frayed, but otherwise he was impeccably dressed. He was a doctor who worked three days a week in Tijuana, where he stayed with his mother and eldest brother, and was on his way home to Santa Ana. He showed me pictures of his children and his wife. We talked about US-Mexican relations, something he knew more about than I did. I probably talked too much about cooking, because we both got hungry. I gave him an orange and some nuts. He offered me a tamale his mother had packed for the trip. When the bus stopped in Santa Ana, I was sorry to see him go.

A few people got off, none got on, and the bus rumbled back onto the highway. I stared out the window into the night, unable to sleep. It was crazy, what I was doing. If I'd stayed in Los Angeles, George would have given me a job in his trailer. Or maybe he would have helped me find something in a real restaurant. There had to be work for a chef in a town where no one ate at home. Yet, there I was, in an over-air-conditioned bus, huddling in my new blanket, which smelled of mildew and street dirt, hurtling through the Mexican night toward an uncertain future.

The rhythm of the bus was bone familiar. I caught fragments of whispered conversations in English, Spanish, and something that sounded like German. I must have dozed, because I dreamed about Antonio, his big eyes dark with love as he smiled at me. He rested his hand on my shoulder, brought his lips to my ear, and whispered, *Tú eres mi amor precioso. Adiós.*

I woke with damp eyes. It came to me that in all those years, drunk and sober, I'd never said good-bye to Antonio. Maybe I ended up with an asshole like Rick to punish myself for still being alive. I'd felt dead when I met Rick, and sex with him had made me feel something again. And after those dark days spent in the shadow of Antonio's death, when I stumbled through Mexico raging at God, I couldn't believe in anything as sweet as real love. I closed my eyes and sent an answer into the darkness. *Sí, my beautiful Antonio, you were also my precious love. Adiós.*

It was neither the time nor the place, and I couldn't remember the words, but I did my best to whisper Kaddish, the prayer for the dead, and wondered why I hadn't thought to do it before.

We rode through the night, the day, and another night before pulling into Tepic. I stepped out into quiet streets bathed in cool blue, predawn light. A sleepy teenager sold *tortas* from a cart. After days of travel food, the hot eggs, beans, and salsa in a roll tasted like heaven. The next bus to Puerto Vallarta left in an hour from the second-class platform. It was a chicken bus, slow and cheap, that would stop for anyone standing along the winding coastal road. With only a hundred miles to go, it was good to be moving along.

I stuffed the blanket and what was left of my food in the top of my pack and sat near the front. After the second stop I had to abandon my seat to an old lady and her two-year-old granddaughter as the bus filled with people on their way to work or family or a doctor's appointment. Not many chickens or goats on the chicken buses anymore, but the press of bodies and the smell of food, dirty baby diapers, and last night's beer made for a pungent ride. After thirty-some hours sitting, it felt good to stand in the aisle and sway with the bus. Hope rose in me with the sun, which, when it appeared over the mountain behind us, struck the ocean with light that sparkled along the tops of the waves.

By the time we got to Puerto Vallarta, the town was alive with morning business. I stepped off the bus and walked toward the waterfront. A voice called my name, and I turned to see Pedro, the produce vendor who had come down from the mountains every morning to deliver a truck full of vegetables to the trailer. I strode over to meet him, feeling more at home than I had anywhere else since I left, a month and a lifetime ago.

Chapter Thirteen

Ty lived with his girlfriend in a studio apartment up the hill from the Malecon. I climbed a few dozen concrete steps up the hill, then a dozen more inside his building, and knocked on his door. My watch said it was nine. If this was like any other day, Ty would be back from the early-morning meeting and busy at work on his computer. I hadn't figured out what exactly he did for a living, but it had something to do with Web page design and online booking for local hotels and resorts.

He answered the door wearing light cotton pajama pants and an old Grateful Dead T-shirt. With his bare feet and long hair, he looked like the old hippie he was.

"Amigo!" He wrapped me in a bear hug. "Your dad wrote you were coming, but he didn't say when."

I shrugged out of my heavy pack. "I've been traveling for days. Do you suppose I could take a shower? Señor Hermanez at the hotel said I could have a job bartending anytime I wanted. I think I better clean up before I go down and see him."

Ty stepped back and waved me into the room. "Fuck yes, you can have a shower. You look and smell like crap. But we're gonna have to talk about the whole bartending thing. Sounds self-destructive."

I shrugged. "It's a job."

"We'll talk." He shooed me toward the bathroom.

I stripped off clothes made ripe by three days on the road and stepped into the shower. Warm water felt fantastic. I found soap, a washcloth, even shaving cream and a razor. I peeled off layers of grime and stubble. By the time I finished, I felt whole for the first time in days. I wrapped a towel around my waist and stumbled back out of the bathroom in search of my pack and some clean clothes.

Ty looked up from his computer. "Now I recognize you. Get dressed, and I'll take you to brunch."

As we walked the few blocks to the all-you-can-eat vegetarian restaurant where Ty ate most of his meals, I filled him in on the past couple of weeks. Between bankruptcy, Rick, the trip down, and of course, John's call, there was a lot to tell.

"And now you've come back to Mexico in search of true love." Ty waved to the waitress as we entered. They chatted for a few minutes in Spanish about her mother's health and the weather before Ty led me to the food bar and handed me a plate. I filled it with beans, eggs, and *chilaquiles*—fried tortillas and salsa—and followed Ty back to his favorite table by the door.

"I don't know, maybe." I savored the feeling of eating hot food at a table with real forks and knives. Nothing like a long road trip to ramp up one's appreciation for the simple things. "I hardly know the guy, but I feel drawn to him like, I don't know, like it's meant to be somehow. Maybe that's crazy. But I'm telling you, nothing else makes sense."

Ty raised his eyebrows. "You think this is a fate thing?"

I shrugged. "Maybe. Can I tell you something really weird without you thinking I'm insane?"

Ty smiled. "Sure. Can't promise about the crazy thing, though. Some of my best friends are nuts."

I took a deep breath. "The thing is, I dreamed about him before we even met. Over and over again, every night for weeks, this guy who looked like John. He'd be walking out of the ocean. I called him my merman. And it was John. I couldn't see his face in the dreams, not until after I knew him. But it was him. I know it was. Or maybe I'm remembering wrong and it wasn't, because that's too weird, isn't it? But I swear, when I saw him in real life, I knew him."

"Stranger things have happened." Ty studied me for a moment. "Okay, let's say he's your dream guy, your merman. What if you don't find him? Or you do, and the whole fated thing turns out to be bull?"

I pushed beans around my plate. "The truth is, there's nothing for me up north. The life I want to live doesn't seem to exist there."

"Spoken like a true expat." Ty pointed at me with his fork. "But you can't take the bartending gig. It's tempting fate, man."

I shrugged again. "I've got to make a living somehow."

Ty grinned. "I've been asking around. Wait till you see what I've lined up for you."

"You found me a job?" Of course he'd found me a job. Ty was the most well-connected gringo in Puerto Vallarta.

Nodding, he wiped his mouth with a paper napkin and rested his elbows on the table. "Caretaking and cooking at a private resort. It's not in Puerto Vallarta, but it's gorgeous, peaceful, a good place to work on your serenity. You can come up here looking for your merman in your free time."

"Wow. So when do I start?"

Ty looked at his watch. "The next water taxi leaves at one o'clock. We'll have time to catch a meeting before we go."

"We?"

He gestured vaguely in the direction of the beach. "I'm always up for a day trip to Layapa. And that way I can introduce you to your new boss."

***

As we walked down the beach, we passed a table full of Americans who were ordering Bloody Marys and daiquiris. Clearly on vacation, they were loud and drunk at noon. The waiter's smile fell away as soon as he turned his back on them. Ty and I exchanged a glance. I was glad to be done with those days.

Moored boats bounced in the bay. Ty pointed toward a white one with a blue awning. LAYAPA WATER TAXI was stenciled on the side.

"You got me a job on an island?" I stared as the boat pitched in the waves.

Ty chuckled. He still wore the loose cotton pants and tee. He'd bundled his hair in a tie-dyed bandanna. Fortunately we wouldn't be attempting any border crossings—he looked like a man with pockets full of hashish. I guess you can take the drugs out of the man, but you can't make a regular guy out of a stoner.

"Not an island. A village, down the coast." He nodded toward the bobbing boat. "There's no road through the mountains. This is the only way to get there." He must have seen the apprehension in my face, because he patted my arm. "Don't worry, amigo. The boats go back and forth to Puerto Vallarta all the time. While you search for your merman, you'll have room, board, and a little cash." He glanced over his shoulder at the loud band of drunks. "And you won't have to serve drinks."

We watched a thin man run bundles, packages, crates, and gasoline jugs down to the boat. A crowd formed at the water's edge. The next load included my pack. As I watched it travel toward the boat, a wave of sadness passed through me. "I'll never find him. I should have stayed in Los Angeles."

Ty laughed. "Are you kidding? I'm taking you to paradise. As for the rest, let the universe take care of it, man, 'cause there's nothing else you can do."

I followed Ty into the water. The sand squished cool, then warm, then wet between my toes. The boat faced us, stern first, as it slapped up and down in the surf. A wave of cold water hit my shins, and the captain held out his hand as I hurled myself up into the boat. I clambered over several bench seats and settled into the second one back. The margarita-fueled revelers crawled in behind me. I was one of the only passengers carrying more than a day-pack. A young man sprang to the bow and stood amid the piles of packages, holding on to a rope. As the boat started to move, the bow tipped up, and it occurred to me that the captain wouldn't be able to see what was ahead. I hoped he and the young navigation officer balancing in front had great communication strategies.

We turned south. With a jolt, I realized we'd be passing the secluded section I thought of as belonging to John and me. The boat reached the boulder at the end of the beach, and there it was, a tiny hidden cove. From out on the water it looked smaller, less private than it had felt when I'd kissed my merman there. That aching sadness in my chest grew. It felt like I was leaving him all over again. I watched until the beach disappeared behind us. Jungle-covered mountains rose up behind the resorts and condominiums. I could see where the road south ended and the white hacienda-style mansions and hotels gave way to thick jungle from shore to mountaintop.

We rode for an hour, the bow rising and falling in brutally back-punishing waves. My ass went numb. The woman on the bench across from me, whose turquoise nail polish appeared to disguise a serious case of fungus, shrieked with each butt-slapping dive. The wind blew ocean smells into us. I licked my lips and tasted salt. We rounded a bend into a cove. A village appeared, carved into the jungle up two steep mountain slopes. The valley was split in half by a river that flowed into the ocean. On one side, white and green umbrellas spanned a long beach. Behind them was an enclave of thatched huts, kitschy enough they had to be a hotel. On the other side of the river sat the bulk of the village, a hillside covered in an architectural mishmash of concrete, stone, and wood. The boat pulled up to a concrete pier.

Ty walked me through town, pointing out the tiny grocery store, a café, some open-air restaurants that consisted of tables set up in their backyards, and a gnarled old tree where he said chickens roosted at night. The streets were paved with an array of concrete slabs and stones. We stood aside as a man led a bundle-laden donkey past us, the animal's hooves clicking rhythmically along the road.

"No cars," Ty explained. "The mountains behind us are impassable, and the only way in is by boat."

Except for the occasional ATV and the bathing suit-clad tourists, it felt like stepping back in time. We passed out of town and kept walking up. The sound of flowing water grew, and the air cooled. We rounded a bend, and there was a waterfall. A few people splashed in the water below the fall. At the pool's edge, other gringos milled around, chatting and taking pictures. Vendors called to them from booths, selling souvenirs and artisan work.

Ty led me toward a wooden gate, above which a sign read LA CASA DE LA SERENIDAD. I looked at Ty. He grinned. The house of serenity. *Huh*. I could use some of that.

As the gate opened, we heard a bell ring in the distance. Stone steps led up through the jungle. As we climbed, the noise of tourists talking disappeared, although we could still hear the rush of cascading water. I was beginning to run out of breath when the vegetation parted, and we found ourselves in a small clearing. Ahead of us was a large building nestled into the mountainside. A network of pathways led to smaller buildings scattered across the hillside. I turned to look back and gasped. Below us lay the village, the river, the beach, and the vast stretch of Pacific Ocean.

"Nice place, eh?" Ty asked.

I nodded, not taking my eyes off the breathtaking view. "It's like a postcard."

I was startled by a deep-throated, feminine laugh. "Makes you understand why the indigenous people didn't distinguish between the sacred and the everyday world. Their everyday world looked pretty darned sacred."

I turned to see a middle-aged woman with long, blondish hair, wearing a colorful skirt, a bikini top, and dozens of beaded necklaces, some of which hung down to her bejeweled belly button. She held out her hand. "I'm Karina. You must be David."

Her hand was as warm and firm as her smile, and I instantly liked her. "This is your place? It's gorgeous."

"It's impossible for a foreigner to actually own anything here. The whole complex is built on leased land. But for all intents and purposes, at least for the immediate future, it's mine. Welcome." She turned to Ty and gave him a quick hug. "Come in, both of you. I made some tea."

She led us into a large space that was more like a covered patio than a room. Columns held up the roof on the ocean side, which was completely open to the air and had the same amazing view. Cupboards spanned the back wall. A long counter in front of them looked like it hid an open kitchen. In the center of the room sat two long tables surrounded by chairs. Comfortable-looking wicker couches and chairs were clustered along the far wall. We followed Karina to those. I sat in one of the chairs. Ty took one end of a couch. A teapot and three mismatched mugs sat on an end table in the center. Karina poured tea and handed us cups before settling herself onto the other end of the couch.

"Ty tells me you went to cooking school in New York." She said it conversationally, but I could feel the signal—we'd plunged into a job interview.

I straightened. This looked like paradise, and it sure as hell beat working the bar in Puerto Vallarta or one of George's tin boxes in Los Angeles. "Yes. The Culinary Institute. If you have access to the Internet, I can find you reviews of the restaurant I ran in Portland."

She cocked her head and looked at me. "Why do you want to work down here in the middle of nowhere?"

All the *right* answers swirled in my head. *I'm looking for a change. To get away from the rat race. I need to simplify my life…* No use trying to spin my past. My bankruptcy was as easy to Google as the reviews. "I made some bad choices, trusted the wrong people…person…and I need somewhere safe to rethink my life."

Her face split into an enormous smile. "Perfect. That's exactly what this place is all about." My surprise must have shown, because she continued, "I built it as a place of transformation. Groups come through for therapy, meditation, recovery, all kinds of healing workshops—some are pretty out-there, others more traditional. I have a yoga teacher on staff and a handful of massage therapists on call. Experts of all sorts come down and lead weeklong retreats."

I looked across the dining room to the view of the river as it flowed between the mountains, across the beach, and into the sea. "This looks like a great place to do that." Karina was watching me. I took a deep breath and went for broke. "It's gorgeous here. If you have work for me, I'd love to stay."

"Most of the retreats are all-inclusive. We feed them three meals a day. I had a local woman cooking, but her husband got a job farther inland, and they're moving next week. Which is fine, since I'd like to have someone living here who speaks English and can manage the place this summer. We don't run groups after March but do get occasional visitors willing to sweat it out." She smiled. "I like the summer myself, nice and hot without many tourists, but my daughter in Connecticut is six months pregnant, so I'm going up there this year."

"Congratulations. You don't look old enough to be a grandma." She nodded her thanks, and I continued, "I'm fine with the heat and would love to stay. I take it your yoga teacher also takes off all summer, since she's already on staff and would be a logical replacement."

"Oh, no, he's here year-round." She frowned. "But meet-and-greet hospitality isn't really his thing. I don't think I could pay him enough for that job. You'll understand when you get to know him." She stood and gestured toward the kitchen. "Let me show you around."

As I'd expected, behind the counter were sinks, two stoves, shelves of pots, pans, and plates—a simple but efficient kitchen. An opening in the back wall led to a pantry area with a large refrigerator, jugs of bottled water, and a giant oven. A small bedroom was visible through an open doorway off the pantry.

Karina pulled the door open, revealing a neatly made single bed and a rough bureau. "It isn't much, but it's free."

I nodded, and she led me back into the pantry. She opened the refrigerator and glanced at me apologetically. "The challenge here is to cook interesting meals with limited ingredients. There's a farmer from up in the hills who comes down every few days with eggs, potatoes, squash, and whatever else is in season. Everything else has to come in on a boat. I send someone in to Puerto Vallarta once a week with a grocery list. We don't have a group this week, so we're getting by on what's available in town." She opened the door wider so I could see inside. "Which isn't much."

I considered the contents: cream, eggs, a block of cheese and another of butter, half an onion, a few peppers, tortillas, and a glass container of cooked rice. Karina looked at her watch. I checked my own. There was a strong possibility I was still being interviewed. I shut the refrigerator door and looked around the pantry. On one of the shelves a bowl held oranges, lemons, limes, and a papaya.

I smiled at Karina. "Shall I make us some lunch?"

She gave me a brisk nod. "Make yourself at home. Holler if you need anything. I'll be catching up on the Puerto Vallarta gossip with Ty."

Once she was gone, I gave myself a few minutes to familiarize myself with the sparsely stocked kitchen, finding the basics: flour, salt, baking soda and powder, uncooked rice, dried beans, cornmeal, potatoes, a smattering of spices. I started making a mental list of things I'd need to feel ready to feed a large group on short notice but stopped myself, realizing I didn't have the job yet and had better get to work. There was no doubt in my mind that my employment hinged on the quality of lunch.

Soup and salad, I decided. Simple but elegant. I began gathering ingredients—the onion, potatoes, a can of chicken stock, and the cream—and carried them out of the pantry to the long, open kitchen area. Karina and Ty sat chatting in the wicker chairs. Even though they didn't look up, I felt exposed cooking out in the open. If I wanted this job—and one look at the view from my kitchen counter told me I did—then I'd better get used to it.

I got the potatoes boiling and went back into the pantry to see what I could find for a salad. Again I carried my ingredients out into the open and began chopping. I found an ancient food processor on a shelf below the counter. I thought I'd seen mint growing in a pot near the front door. Taking a pair of scissors with me, I went outside to gather some.

Thirty-seven minutes after she'd left the pantry, I called to Karina and Ty that lunch was ready. She looked pleased when she saw the two places set at the counter using festive mats and napkins I'd found in the pantry. I'd rolled the napkins and set them in the center of the place mats, each held together with a twisted mint stem. I'd set a pitcher of lemon water between Ty and Karina.

Ty's eyebrows rose as he uncurled the mint stem from his napkin. "That's pretty slick, man. Fancy."

I smiled and set before them plates with bowls of creamy, white potato soup, swirled with butter. I had surrounded the bowls with bright fruit and rice salad drizzled in rich golden dressing and decorated with sunbursts of mint leaves. "Warm vichyssoise with papaya, rice, and mint salad with a honey-lime dressing. Bon appétit."

Karina's eyes were wide. "It's so pretty I hate to touch it."

Ty tasted a spoonful of soup. He groaned. "That's incredible."

Karina looked up at me. "You do know I can't pay much. Room and board and a few thousand pesos a month. Consuela sometimes got tips." She looked down at her plate. "I bet you'd get more. But it still wouldn't be enough."

I laughed. "Don't you think you'd better taste the food before you hire me?"

"I don't have to. All I have to do is watch him." She nodded toward Ty who was alternately shoveling in food and making groaning, moaning noises.

"He's my friend, and he doesn't want me sleeping on his couch." I gestured toward her plate. "So eat. If you like it, we can talk about the job."

Obediently she bit into a forkful of salad. My shoulders relaxed as I watched her face. When she could talk again, she asked, "Are you sure you don't want to find somewhere better to work? You certainly could."

I looked past her at the green hills and the wide expanse of ocean. A bird called from nearby. I shook my head. "My life has been out of control lately. I could use some *serenidad*. I haven't felt this peaceful in a long time."

"I'm not one to look a gift horse in the mouth." She thrust her hand across the table. "You're hired. We can discuss the details later."

I shook her hand. "Thank you. I'll do the best I can for you."

I heard a familiar voice calling, "Karina? I'm going down to the village. You need anything?"

Karina brightened. "Oh, good, you can meet our yoga teacher."

I froze and stared unbelieving as John walked through the door.

Chapter Fourteen

I vaguely heard Karina speaking to him. He was looking at me. It felt like the air had been sucked out of the room, which was crazy because it only had three walls. I couldn't breathe, and I didn't know if it was from shock or because I was waiting for him to react. Sound exploded again as all four of us talked at once.

Ty started it with, "See what I told you, man? The universe provides. It's all good."

And John said, "David?"

And I said, "But you're on an island somewhere."

And Karina said, "You guys know each other?"

I stared into his sea-green eyes and whispered, "Yes."

John looked back, his gaze soft. "I thought you were in Los Angeles."

"I came back."

Karina cleared her throat. "How about if you show David around the complex, John, while Ty and I finish our lunch?"

A smile slowly spread across John's face. "You're the new cook?"

I glanced toward the counter where Karina was studiously concentrating on her salad. Ty had stopped eating and was beaming a self-satisfied smile.

I looked at John. "Let's go. I'm anxious to see the rest of this place."

He gestured toward the door and said in that lovely, deep voice, "I'm right behind you."

That sent a shiver to my bones.

Once we were out the door and into the little clearing, I turned toward John. He put a finger to his lips, grabbed my hand, and started hauling me up a set of stone steps dug into the hillside. I thought I might be dreaming, but his hand was steady and real in mine. I felt the chatter of unanswered questions building in my head, but I took a deep breath, resolved to savor the moment, the sight and feel of him so near, and followed him up the mountain. We passed a few of the huts I'd seen before. The path turned around the last of them and flattened out. John stopped and turned to face me.

He was smiling. One of his teeth was crooked. I'd never noticed. But then I'd never seen him like this, his face open and happy. Even the wrinkle of sadness around his eyes looked lighter.

He ran his hand across my scalp, his gaze fixed on my mouth as he asked, "Are you really here?"

"My father said you called."

He cupped my face. "As soon as Frank gave me the message, but it was too late. I didn't think I'd ever see you again."

"I would have contacted someone else, but there weren't any other numbers in your phone."

John shrugged. "Who else would I call?"

"Paul?" I looked up at his chin.

"No, not Paul." He sounded sad and tired. I leaned in and kissed him.

He tasted sweet, and the kiss started that way too, his lips soft against mine. I groaned, leaning into him, opening my mouth for his tongue, and like a match igniting a gas flame, the heat erupted between us. His clothes were made of soft cotton that let me feel the long bands of muscle along his back. When I felt the tight globes of his ass shudder beneath my hands, I pulled him close as if to climb inside his beautiful skin. He held my face, deepening the kiss, and ground against me. The feel of his hard cock, even through all those clothes, was explosive, and I thrust back.

John pulled away, leaning his forehead against mine. I rested my hands on his hips. My breath in the space between us sounded like I'd been running. So did his.

He whispered, "I'm supposed to be showing you the complex."

I closed my eyes and concentrated on the feel of his hands on my shoulders. "Do you live here?"

He nodded, jostling my head as he did.

I pulled back and waited until I could look into his eyes before asking, "Maybe you could show me your room first?"

That big smile returned, and once more his hand was gripping mine, and we were almost running along the path, then climbing farther up the hillside.

"That's it." He pointed to an ancient-looking hut. As we neared, I saw that it was a small, open-sided building with hip-high stone walls, cement pillars, and a palm leaf-thatched roof.

John pulled me up the last few steps and into the hut through an opening in the stone wall. To one side there was a blue-tiled kitchen open to the jungle. It had a propane tank hooked to a two-burner stove top. A giant plastic water jug sat on the counter.

"Welcome to my house." He looked around a little self-consciously. "It isn't fancy. No electricity or running water—there's an outhouse in the back, but I have to shower at Karina's."

Bougainvillea bloomed along one side of the stone wall. I looked out at the view. The entire valley spread below us. We could see the ocean, the town, and the river running through the center. "It's beautiful."

I turned toward the room, and my attention was riveted by a bed. Covered in mosquito netting, the bed swung from the rafters.

John rested his hand on my back. "How did you find me? Did Frank tell you I was in Layapa?"

"I haven't seen him since I got back to Mexico. I thought you lived on an island out there somewhere." I waved in the general direction of the Pacific. "I came to Layapa for the job."

His breath on my face was warm. "And you're staying?"

I nodded.

"I'm glad."

He held my face. "Here's something I never expected to see—David Schwartz, in the flesh, in my room."

My stomach grumbled—I'd made lunch but hadn't eaten. "Speaking of flesh, I don't suppose you have anything to eat here, do you?"

He shrugged. "Not much. I really do have to go to the village today and stock up. There are still some lentils." He walked into the kitchen, lifted the lid from a red, plastic cooler, and produced a lidded pot. After scooping a ladleful of thick green glop into a chipped ceramic bowl, he handed it to me, along with a spoon.

I stared at the contents. It looked and smelled like lentils. Just lentils. Cold lentils. No flavorings, additions, or—I tasted a spoonful—salt. I tried to nod my thanks. I was really hungry, and I hated to offend him. I tried another bite. John was looking at me expectantly. I chewed and swallowed, feeling the bolus of tasteless food clogging my esophagus on the way down.

"It's better warm." My face must have betrayed me, because John sounded defensive.

He handed me a glass of water, and I chugged it to wash away the taste, or lack of it. I handed him back the bowl. "I'm sorry, John. I don't mean to be rude. It's that food is… well, it's what I do. I'll cook for you, and you'll see."

He scraped the lentils back into the pot and set it in the cooler. He stepped forward and touched my hand. His touch was light and sent a shiver up my arm. "Obviously I'm not immune to the pleasures of the flesh. But I don't need to add gluttony to my list of sins."

Gluttony? I gaped at him. I opened my mouth to argue but stopped. I didn't want our first fight to be about fucking, tasteless lentils. So I shrugged and turned to look out at the view. "I should get down there to meet with Karina, say good-bye to Ty."

"The boat back to Puerto Vallarta leaves in a few hours. You have time. I need to go soon, though. It's not only the groceries. I promised to check that the church was ready for Mass. The priest only comes once a month and will be here on Sunday." He gave an apologetic shrug. "It's one of the few ways I'm allowed to help."

I stared for a moment. I didn't even know how to start that conversation. John grasped my shoulders and turned me again to look out over the valley. He pressed into my back and pointed down the hill. "I'm supposed to be showing you around. All the smaller, thatch-roofed huts are guest houses. I doubt you'll need to deal with them at all. Consuela, who cooked before you, didn't. Maria comes up from town to clean, do the linens, and whatnot. There's a storage building over there by the main building—see the tin roof? The only things you might care about in there are the extra towels and the washing machine and dryer. During the dry season we can hang the laundry out on those lines"—he gestured toward a series of clotheslines white with flapping sheets—"but during the wet season you'll thank God every day for the dryer."

"Where do you teach?" I asked, scanning the complex for something that could pass for a recreation building or yoga studio.

John pointed to a large, flat patio shaded by tall trees. "If it rains, we can move the furniture around in the dining room, but mostly we're down there." He kissed the crook of my neck.

I leaned into him, wrapping his arm around my chest. "John?"

"Uh-huh?" He was nuzzling my neck again.

"You're really different here. Do you know that?"

He jerked back. "Am I? In a bad way?"

"No, no." I pulled him closer. "It's good. You're more... I don't know, *relaxed* isn't the right word. Happy? At ease? It's nice. It's also a little confusing."

He took a breath so deep I felt his chest expand behind me. Letting it out slowly, he loosened his grasp on me. I turned toward him. He was staring out across the valley. After a moment, he brought his gaze to mine. "I told you I'm not comfortable with casual relationships. Now that you're here, it feels good to have time. That makes me happy. Now I should let you get back to Karina."

As we started out the door, John stopped. "She'll probably want you around through dinner. Can you come back here after that?"

I smiled. "Of course. In the meantime, Ty is going to want to talk with me about you. Is that a problem?"

His brow furrowed. "Why would it be?"

I shrugged. "Maybe you don't want everyone knowing your business?"

He locked me with his oceanic gaze again. "I gave up secrets. They're crippling."

***

Karina had her back to a pillar, and Ty was dangling his feet over the open-air edge of the dining room. It was an interesting way to sunbathe. They both looked up when I came in.

"How was the tour?" Karina's smile was just short of a smirk.

I turned toward the back. "I'll get the kitchen cleaned up."

"I'm way ahead of you," Ty called. "Can't cook for shit, but I'm good with the dishes."

I stopped and glanced over my shoulder. "Oh, um, then if it's okay with you, Karina, I'll get myself some lunch."

She waved me toward the counter. "Sure, knock yourself out."

Ty had put the soup pot on a lower shelf. I decided to leave that for later. Vichyssoise really is better cold.

"You'll need to stop at the store this afternoon." Karina's voice carried from the other room. "I can't wait to see what you do with more choices."

I poked my head out of the pantry. "Sure, no problem."

They were now both sitting at the counter, watching me.

Ty winked. "You like the job perks?"

Karina laughed. I felt myself starting to blush, so I ducked back into the pantry to forage for food. Something simple and quick—I was hungry enough to consider John's baby puke-colored lentils.

There was nothing faster than a quesadilla. I brought out the tortillas, cheese, and a sliced pepper for garnish. Karina and Ty watched me work for a minute before Karina asked, "You're the guy John's been running over to see in Puerto Vallarta?"

I looked at Ty. He shrugged. I focused again on Karina. "John told you about us?"

She snorted. "I was guessing. John's not big on confessional conversations, which is sort of ironic, don't you think?"

I laughed.

She leaned her elbows on the counter. "I thought something must be going on. In three years he's used my phone maybe a dozen times, and suddenly he's asking if he can recharge his cell down here? That and the overnights in Puerto Vallarta had me pretty convinced he was seeing someone."

I watched cheese slide off my knife and onto the tortilla. "That would be me."

There was a silence.

I cleared my throat. "It's not a problem, is it? I mean, if I, we…"

"Is he the reason you applied for this job?" She was watching me intently.

I started. "Shit, no. I thought he lived on some island, and when I saw his phone only had one contact number—mine—I worried he might have a partner somewhere he was cheating on." She kept looking at me, and I decided she'd only believe the absolute truth. I set down my knife. "Honestly, I walked in here hoping to get a job where I could support myself while I kept searching for him. And that's crazy because we haven't known each other that long. But it feels right. So if it's going to be a problem for me to work here and be involved with John, I'll have to find other work somewhere in town, because while I didn't come here expecting to see him, I came back to Mexico hoping I would."

She gestured toward Ty. "That's what he said, but as you said, he's your friend, and he wants you off his couch, and he knows I'm a sucker for a love story, so I had to be sure. It's about time John had someone fierce for him. It will be good to see him happy again. I was getting worried. These past few weeks he's been almost as reclusive as when Paul left. Like a bear, he is, crawling into his cave whenever it hurts."

Oh, right, Paul—the guy John loved more than God. I focused on assembling my lunch and told myself it didn't matter that Paul was John's one who got away—I could be the one who stayed.

Chapter Fifteen

I offered to walk Ty to the pier and get groceries on the way back.

As soon as we were out the door, I said, "You knew John was here."

Ty shrugged. "I heard there was an ex-priest teaching yoga at Karina's. How many of them can there be kicking around? I thought it was worth a chance."

"Why didn't you tell me?"

He started down the path. "Right. And have you all heartbroken if I was wrong? No way, man."

I followed him down the hill. The day felt like a miracle.

As we neared the dock, Ty put a hand on my arm to stop me. "I think you should think about whether you'd want this job without him here. I mean, love's great and all, but if you're feeling like you're working way below your pay grade—which you will be—it could start to wear unless there are other things that make the job worth your time."

I frowned at him. "Wait, aren't you the one who brought me here?"

"Yep. And even without the merman, there are lots of reasons to like it here. But you need to work out for yourself what's gonna do it for you." He gestured up the hill toward the resort. "When you get up there, Karina's going to sit you down and talk about the job in detail. It might be worth your while to think about what you want to bargain for. You blew her away with lunch. Shit, you blew me away. That was some fine food. She can't pay you much, but she'll probably give you whatever she can—days off, a better room, maybe a local kid to help out, fucking mints on your pillow—I don't know. You're good. You may be in retreat right now, but that doesn't mean you need to feel like you're begging."

I looked across the water at the beach, its golden sand dotted with big striped umbrellas. "It feels really good to be here. I want to see what happens with John. But you're right. I should think about it all before I walk back up the hill."

Ty patted my back. "Don't forget to drop by a meeting whenever you're in town. And call if it gets rough. Karina's got a phone, so there's no excuse."

The water taxi bounced in the waves next to the pier. The captain started motioning for people to board.

I hugged Ty. "Thanks for bringing me here."

"No problem, brother. Stay cool."

I waved and watched the boat pull away before I turned to walk up the hill through town. This time I paid more attention to the houses and shops along the way. There were a few small restaurants, an odds-and-ends store, and a tiny tourist shop. I stepped into a grocery, which consisted of two dark rooms filled with everything from fresh produce to bar soap. I filled my basket with eggs, milk, more cream, a bag of peppers, three beautiful yellow squash, and a handful of tomatoes. A woman who looked to be in her forties sat behind the counter, watching me as I perused a shelf of dried spices.

I wished her good day. Which started a long conversation about the weather, the tourists, and the difficulties of running a grocery in a remote village. While she tallied my groceries, she asked what I was doing in town and seemed startled when I told her I was the new cook at La Casa de la Serenidad.

She nodded in the direction of the resort. "I thought she was hiring a gringo for that."

"I am a gringo." I sent a silent kiss toward Antonio's ghost.

As Ty had predicted, Karina was waiting for me in the dining room. I made a deal with her—I'd take the job, low pay and all, as long as I got help with the dishes and complete charge of the kitchen. It might have been a small resort without prestige, but as I unpacked my knives in the dark pantry and hung up my white jacket, I staked my claim not as the cook but as the chef.

***

The sunset bloomed across the ocean as I climbed to John's hut after cleaning up from dinner. The faint beat of a classic rock song carried on the wind from the beach. I heard the rustling of small animals, the occasional chirp of a bird. I paused to catch my breath and looked up toward the hut. A candle inside a glass chimney burned on the low stone wall. Beside it, John stood watching me. He wore a long-sleeved shirt open like a jacket, and his torso glowed in the candlelight. His shirt fluttered in the breeze, and the whole scene looked like something out of a cheesy, romantic movie. I almost expected to hear orchestra music swelling in the background.

A donkey brayed in the distance, and it felt real again, not a tropical paradise but rural, coastal Mexico, where the streets smelled of dog shit and burning garbage. I climbed the last few steps. John stepped in front of the light, his arms outstretched, and I had a sudden flash of memory. I'd dreamed him like this. Or I'd made him into the man in my dreams. Either way it was hot.

I wrapped my arms around him. John's lips came down hot on mine. His cock pressed hard into my belly. Anticipation had bubbled through me all evening, and I was half-hard already, myself. John's mouth opened to my tongue. He tasted earthy, probably from some sort of weird yogi herbal tea, and sweet with the promise of passion.

Letting my pack drop, I ran my hands over his finely muscled shoulders and pushed his shirt down until it fell to the floor. I let my fingers graze across the ripple of his abdomen—more like gentle ocean waves than a six-pack but taut beneath my touch. His eyes were hot as he watched me touch him. He hooked his hands under my T-shirt and pulled it off in one long caress. My breath caught.

We both wore loose cotton pants, mine the dark canvas chef's pants I'd worn for the interview, his, soft blue jersey that looked like silk as it draped from his hips and from his cock. I stepped back and slid out of my pants and watched him do the same. He looked strikingly handsome in the candlelight, the clean line of his bones softened by the muscles mounded around them. A thatch of dark hair curled in the center of his chest. I let my eyes travel down his torso to the bed of pubic hair that framed his gorgeous cock. I licked my lips, my hand straying almost automatically to my own cock. John inhaled sharply, and I looked up to see him devouring me with his eyes. He didn't move. I stroked myself a few times, watching him watch me, getting off on his hunger.

He closed his mouth. Eventually he pulled his focus away from my cock and met my gaze. He bit his lip. "I've never seen anyone do that. It's very sexy."

I raised my eyebrows. "Not a big porno watcher?"

He shrugged. "I'm afraid you'll find me an inexperienced lover. Paul and I, well, we weren't exactly adventurous."

I was developing something of a complex about this Paul guy and must have winced at the name, because John stepped forward and pulled me into his arms, his lips sweet against mine, his tongue sliding deep into my mouth. When we broke, he brought his mouth to my ear, his breath hot against my neck as he whispered, "I can't stop remembering what it felt like to be in you. I want to do that again." Blood surged into my cock, and I'm sure he felt me hardening, because he smiled when he looked into my eyes and asked, "Is that okay?"

"Oh yeah." I bent to fumble in the front pocket of my pack. John's hands never left me. He stroked my back, my head, my ass, his touch gentle and relentless, not stopping even as I retrieved a condom and lube pillow and stood back up. John held open the mosquito netting for me. I was barely through when I felt him behind me, his skin warm against my own as he pushed me farther onto the bed, which swung beneath us.

He started to roll off. I held his arm to keep him on top of me. "Like this."

I squeezed the length of his cock with my ass cheeks, and he moaned. God, I wanted it, wanted him. I handed him the condom. He pulled away to put it on, and I reached around and emptied the lube pillow onto my ass. Scooting up a little on my knees, I pushed lube into my asshole with my index finger. I was practically panting, and I heard John's breath coming in little huffs behind me. As soon as I heard the *slap* of unrolled latex against skin, I guided his cock to my ass. He paused with the tip pressed against me. I groaned and pushed back. It was like an ache, this need for him. He must have felt it too, because he thrust hard, pulled back, and plunged in farther until he struck gold and I was writhing beneath him. I twisted my head to catch his mouth in a sloppy kiss. We were both grunting, great, primal sounds that echoed in the jungle around us. Sweat pooled between us and dripped down my sides. My universe condensed to the single point of his cock pounding my ass, hard and fast. I was completely focused on him, his cock stretching my ass, his breath, the way he panted my name, his strong hands grasping my own, holding me to the bed, which was swinging wildly with his thrusts. I felt his orgasm start with the tightening of his toes, rigid against the clench of my own. It moved up our thighs in waves of rippling muscles, and I was pressing into him, forcing him to bury himself totally inside me as I arched back against his chest, calling his name as he held me, my name spilling from his lips as my cock spilled onto the sheets.

John was the first to stir. I winced when he pulled out, and he whispered, "Oh, David, I'm so sorry. Did I hurt you?"

I shook my head and rolled toward him. I ran my hand along his chin until the worry left his eyes. "I lo—" I stopped myself. That was fucking crazy talk. "That was amazing."

John smiled down at me. "What a miracle you are."

I pulled him into a long, sweet kiss.

***

A cacophony of birds woke me. The light was still dim and the bed empty. As I emerged from the mosquito netting, the jungle around the hut sounded alive with birdsong. I inhaled the smell of lush, green vegetation. In the distance, I heard waves crashing against the surf. From the village came the sound of crowing roosters. Down below, a man leading a donkey was wading across the river. The air felt cooler than it had the day before. A breeze brought goose bumps to my arms, and I scrambled to find my clothing.

I spotted John sitting cross-legged on a rock outcropping a hundred feet away. With his hands draped gracefully open on his knees, he looked the picture of tranquility. I figured he'd know where to find me and started down the hill. I smelled like sweat and sex and needed to clean up and get coffee—not necessarily in that order. I looked down at the beach and thought vaguely about running, but I decided I'd better get a feel for the rhythms of the resort before I went off on my own.

The kitchen was exactly as I'd left it. I started the coffee, gathered a change of clothing, and walked across the back courtyard to the tin building that held laundry facilities and the staff bathroom. Winter and spring are the dry seasons in Layapa, and Karina had given me a lecture on water conservation before letting me use the shower the night before. I figured two showers a day would be against the rules, so I made do with a sponge bath and a shave.

Karina was sitting at the counter sipping coffee when I returned. She gave me a big smile. "Thanks for making coffee. I'm a mess without it."

I laughed and poured myself a cup. "Believe me, I understand addiction. How do we set up coffee service when the guests are here? And what would you like for breakfast?"

I made us both eggs and toast, and we talked about feeding the groups. There'd been a last-minute cancellation, which explained the current lack of guests, but after that the resort was fully booked through March. The next group would arrive on Sunday. Karina agreed to spend the morning helping me plan the week's meals.

"Does John ever eat with you?" I asked her as I washed our plates.

"Every now and then. He likes to keep his own schedule." She waved her hand dismissively. "You know, he's got that monastic yogi thing going. I think he lives on lentils and brown rice."

I grimaced. "That reminds me. Are we vegetarian here?"

Karina shook her head. "Depends on the group. This next week is a couples' retreat. We schedule it every year around Valentine's Day. Half the guys are reluctant to come anyway. If we took away their meat, we'd have a lot of empty beds."

I stared at her. Valentine's Day? Did grown-ups celebrate that? Rick hadn't. And Antonio? Well, that was a long time ago. Shit. It was named after a saint too. John was probably used to great things on Valentine's Day. I imagined Paul as the best Valentine's Day boyfriend in history.

Karina must have misunderstood my panic, because she patted my arm. "Don't worry. It'll be a small group, ten couples this year. And about half of them are repeats who we already know are easy to please. Although we will need to go shopping tomorrow."

I nodded, still wondering what to do about Valentine's Day.

Karina continued, "I might as well stay over tomorrow night since the group comes in on Saturday. It works best for transportation if they spend their first night in Puerto Vallarta. We'll come back on the early boat Sunday. If you bring back the groceries tomorrow, you'll have a couple nights alone here. You think you can handle it?"

My ass tingled. It might not be hearts and flowers, but John had been without for a long time before and after Paul, so maybe the weekend together would be Valentine's present enough.

***

At the last minute John announced he was going to Puerto Vallarta with us. He smiled and picked up an armful of empty shopping bags. "I'll help carry."

Karina and I had split the grocery list. She had errands to do out by the airport. She'd volunteered to take a cab out to the big-box stores, stock up on some staples, and meet me at the consulate to fill out the forms for my work visa before John and I had to be back at the pier for the afternoon boat. I tucked my half of the list into my back pocket. I was in charge of fresh food. I planned to contact a few of the vendors I'd worked with for the movie to see what they had that looked good. I also wanted to catch a meeting. Having John along was a bonus.

The ocean was calm as glass, and the trip took half the time it had when Ty brought me down. Karina sat next to the captain, and they chatted about the tourist season and the weather. John and I sat near the front. His thigh felt delicious pressed against mine. I leaned into him every time he pointed toward the shore and shouted out an anecdote about a passing place.

As the boat neared shore, a few gringo passengers bent to untie their sneakers. I'd been reminded of the landing by Karina and John and had already rolled my pants to my knees and tucked my flip-flops in my day pack. When the bow hit the sandy beach, I jumped down and raised a hand to help John, who didn't need it but was gracious enough to pretend he did. The whole transaction made me feel like a native, like I belonged. I turned toward the boardwalk, realizing this was the spot where I'd first seen John disembark. A lot could happen in a few months.

Karina hopped in a cab and drove off, waving.

"Come on." John strode down the sidewalk away from the beach.

I trotted to catch up with him. "Where are we going?"

He smiled at me over his shoulder. "To the clinic."

I picked up my pace. For an inexperienced guy, he was doing a better job of thinking ahead than I was.

By the time we loaded all the supplies onto the afternoon boat, I'd reconnected with a handful of vendors, introduced John to my favorite Puerto Vallarta tamale stand, hit a meeting while John went to Mass, and filled out paperwork that would allow me to work in Layapa indefinitely. And amid the dozen or so bags of coffee, meat, produce, tortillas, and pasta were two shiny new clean bills of health. It was starting to feel like a new beginning.

Chapter Sixteen

On the boat, John greeted a group of women who were spending the winter in Layapa and had taken a number of classes from him. They talked him into giving them a private yoga class before dinner. He lifted his eyebrows in question to me. I shrugged. We had most of the weekend alone together. I wasn't going to begrudge them an hour or two.

As Karina had promised, a middle-aged man named Ricardo met us at the dock with his two donkeys. I introduced myself as the new chef, and we shook hands. John and I helped load up the animals and followed them up to the resort. The women scattered to change. At the resort, we piled bags of food on the kitchen counter. Ricardo left with his donkeys. John left to change for class, and I was alone in my kitchen with a mountain of food to put away.

I reorganized the shelves as I stocked them, claiming the space and setting up for a work flow I could enjoy. As I worked, I thought about dinner. Since I hadn't been able to think of anything to get him for Valentine's Day, I wanted to make something special for dinner. Not only would it be my gift to John, but it would give me a chance to get to know the kitchen without pressure. Glancing around the pantry, I spotted the tortilla griddle. It looked vaguely like a crepe pan. What's more romantic than crepes? I ignored the fact that the delicacy of the task and my lack of proper equipment seemed to forecast failure.

I stockpiled ingredients. I let the eggs rest on the counter, along with a chunk of pale butter. I hadn't made crepes since school where we'd weighed our quantities—one hundred grams of sugar, five of flour. Here in the Mexican jungle, even if I'd had a scale, the humidity would have messed with the weights. I'd need to guess and hope for the best. Doubting John would be up for dessert for dinner, I skipped the sugar and made savory batter. After sorting through the groceries for foods we had in excess, I decided to fill them with spinach and sautéed mushrooms in a béchamel sauce.

The filling was easy. I made it first and let it sit on the stove while I concentrated on the crepes. I turned the tortilla griddle over, exposing its flat underside. After brushing it clean, I put it over the gas burner to heat. Under the counter, I found a bowl and a whisk. I was rooting around hopefully, looking for a sieve, when I heard him.

There he was, looking elegant in his yoga clothes, loose, dark cotton pants and a tight, green tank that matched his eyes. The rush of excitement I felt at his greeting surprised me. I'd seen him less than two hours before.

"Hi." I smiled. "Class over?"

He nodded and stepped closer. "What are you doing?"

I shrugged. "Courting disaster. Trying to make crepes without the proper tools."

He slid onto one of the stools lining the counter. "Can I watch?"

His voice was low as he said it, and I felt a tingle of heat zing through my veins. I remembered stroking my cock for him the night before. I leaned across the counter, bringing my face close to his, and whispered, "If you like."

He blushed, but didn't pull away.

I straightened. Cracking four eggs into the bowl and whisking, I contemplated John's strong hands. "We can postpone dinner, you know. Find something else to fill our time?"

He cocked his head and looked at me. "That's tempting. But I'd like us to spend some time together without sex."

I added the flour and began beating again, the sound of the whisk against the bowl keeping time with my heart. "Is that your polite way of saying you'd like us to stop? 'Cause if it is, what was all that about getting tested today?"

"What?" John blinked at me. "No. No, not at all. The opposite, actually. I want to get to know you. Go deeper." He paused and seemed lost in contemplation of my hand whirling the whisk. He cleared his throat. "It's very beautiful, the way you do that."

I looked down at the bowl and the spinning mass of flour and eggs. "Um, thank you."

"You don't wear a watch."

I shrugged. "I can't stand having anything on my hands or wrists when I'm cooking. And there's always a wall clock in the kitchen."

Neither of us spoke as I added more flour and some milk. It felt like the ground had shifted beneath us.

John nodded toward the griddle. "Your pan is smoking."

I jumped, reaching to turn down the burner. I looked at my batter, smooth and thin, the color of sand. I glanced up at John. "I don't have a sieve, so this might be a little lumpy. Would you like to try a crepe?"

He held my gaze. "I want whatever you want to give me."

I swallowed. When I spoke, my voice sounded almost an octave lower than usual. "Right. If you'd like to get to know me, you're going to have to eat." I slathered the griddle with butter and poured on a dollop of batter, keeping up my patter to restrain myself from falling into those clear, green eyes. "It won't be perfect. I don't have a spreader, and this spatula isn't doing the job. I hope you don't mind some unevenness in your crepe."

He smiled. "I'm not looking for perfection, David."

I gazed at him, his chiseled features and wavy hair, the way his bones moved beneath his skin and the graceful curve of his muscles. He was pretty damned close to perfect. I jiggled the griddle until the pancake moved. I flicked my wrist. The crepe spun in a perfect arc and landed flat with a satisfying *slap*.

I frowned. "I don't want to hear any garbage about gluttony either. God gave you taste buds for a reason." I slid the crepe onto a plate, spread on the filling, and rolled it into a thick cylinder. I dribbled a decorative swirl of béchamel sauce along the length. I garnished the plate with slices of mango, shaved cheese, and a sprig of mint and set it in front of him.

John's eyes were wide. "It's like a painting. I don't want to disturb it."

I smiled. "You eat first with your eyes and then your mouth."

His gaze met mine. "I think I can do that."

I swallowed hard and battered up the pan again.

John looked back down at his plate. "This is beautiful. I know where Karina keeps the wine. Should I get some to serve with this?"

I glanced at him, suddenly aware of how little we actually knew each other. "Feel free to pour some for yourself, but none for me, thank you. I'm a recovering alcoholic."

He stared at me and voiced what I was feeling. "Clearly we haven't talked enough yet. Now I understand what you meant by a meeting. I thought you were seeing someone about vegetables."

I flipped my crepe and nodded toward his plate. "Eat while it's hot."

He cut a small sliver and brought it to his mouth. His eyes closed, and a little groan escaped. He opened his eyes and looked at me. "That's incredible. You should be a chef with your own restaurant."

I prepared my plate and came around the counter to sit next to him. "I am a chef, and I had my own restaurant. It went belly-up last fall."

John's eyebrows furrowed. He gestured to his crepe. "But this is so good. How could it fail?"

I took a bite and wondered if walnuts might be a nice addition. Or raisins. I swallowed and looked at John. "There's a line in the AA literature that talks about being spiritually bankrupt. I've had two serious relationships in my life." I shook my head at his raised eyebrows. "I'm not a saint like you—I've been to bed with plenty of guys, but only two could really be considered boyfriends. The first was Antonio. His death left me spiritually bankrupt. I didn't care what, or who, I did after that. More recently, the other, Rick, left me financially bankrupt, and while it sucks big-time, it's a much better way to go."

He rested his hand on my thigh. "I'm so sorry."

I shrugged and pointed at his food. "This is your Valentine's present. So eat."

"Valentine's? I haven't had a valentine since the third grade." He looked at me with alarm. "I didn't even think…"

I shrugged. "It's okay. I only thought of it because of something Karina said. But really, I do want you to eat my food. It will make me happy."

He nodded solemnly and turned back to his plate. "That's very much what I'd like to do."

Later we made love slowly, truly naked together. The first time I came, John took me in his mouth, tonguing the underside of my cock in a way that made me thrust up into him, gasping for breath. Then I closed my mouth over his cock. He tasted like the sea, and I gulped down his cum like a drowning man. The second time I came, it was with his cock buried in my ass, skin to skin and soul to soul.

***

John shook me awake.

I blinked into the darkness. "What time is it?"

"Around five." He took my hand and pulled me up to sit. "I want to show you something."

"What?" I stared at him, fighting my impulse to slap his hand away and fall back onto the bed.

"Come on, David." He stood, and the bed jostled beneath me. "You'll like it, I promise."

Shaking my head, I scooted to the edge of the bed and climbed off. John held out my clothes from the night before. He looked excited, practically bouncing on his toes.

He led me down the path and past the resort. Even though I could barely see, I kept my gaze on the path. The last thing I wanted was to trip and tumble down the mountain in the dark. In the predawn stillness, the waterfall roared. It faded as we walked past the falls and down toward town. John held my hand and steered me onto a path I hadn't been on before. We climbed a steep hill that crested at the edge of town and then sloped down to run along the river. Eventually we were walking on a wide, packed-earth trail.

I heard rustling in the vegetation beside the road, but for the most part, our footfalls were the loudest sound. I inhaled the trail smells of dirt and plants, punctuated by aging donkey piles. We rounded a bend and heard what sounded like dozens of trotting hooves. We stepped off the path as a rider appeared, leading a long string of horses.

"*Hola.*"

He'd passed by the time I mustered my own, "Buenos días."

We'd been walking in the dark for a very long time when John led me off the path and onto a patch of sand. The river sounded close. John shrugged out of the pack he'd been carrying and pulled out a wide blanket, which he spread on the sand.

"We're picnicking?" I sat on the blanket beside him. "Or did you have something more X-rated in mind?"

He lay down and gestured toward the sky. "Look."

I twisted to see where he was pointing. Stars covered the sky in a thick array. I lay down, my shoulder against John's, and looked. "When I was a kid, I used to think that the night sky was a blanket full of holes and that somewhere out there was a giant light shining through."

"Huh. I like that." His hand curled into mine. "And maybe, metaphorically, it's true."

We lay silently for a while, listening to the river and watching the stars.

I turned to look at the vague outline of his profile. "John?"

"Hmm?" He squeezed my hand.

"Was it hard to quit being a priest?"

He was silent so long that I thought he wasn't going to answer. When he did, his voice undulated softly, like the water flowing over rocks in the river. "I was fifteen when I felt the Call. It's still one of my most profound memories, even though I can't be sure how much of it was God and how much the yearning for acceptance of a socially awkward, gay child. Either way, it was the only thing I wanted from life. When I entered the priesthood, the official stance on homosexuality was that it was the act, not the inclination, which was against God's law. In practice, it was more like 'Don't ask, don't tell.' Even in the confessional, I found I could obscure the gender when I confessed to impure thoughts."

I rolled onto my side so I could face him. "Do you think that now? That what we do is a sin?"

I felt more than saw the shake of his head. "No. I struggled with it for a long time and came to believe that only a cruel God would punish me for being who I am. But celibacy is celibacy, so I made my peace with being a priest."

He stopped speaking, and I prompted, "And then?"

The sand crunched as he shifted his position. "And then came the abuse scandals, and the Vatican reacted by forbidding ordination of new gay priests, even though, of course, the one thing has nothing to do with the other, and no gay priests were ever accused of molestation. I began to question whether I could continue on in the Church. In the midst of my soul-searching, I got transferred to a small parish in Minnesota where Paul was the choir director. One thing led to another. I eventually quit."

"Do you miss it?"

"Sometimes." He rolled toward me. I felt his breath on my face. He ran a finger along my brow. "But I'm finding there are some very satisfying compensations." He slid his hand to the back of my neck and pulled me into a long, sweet kiss. When we broke, I heard the amusement in his voice as he assured me, "And I wasn't a very good priest. Toward the end I was angry and miserable. That made me impatient with people. I think I'm a better, or at least happier, yoga teacher."

His lips on mine were soft, and I tried not to think too much about Paul and the compensations he might have provided. I wasn't usually jealous of old lovers, but Frank Wannaker's phrase *loved him more than God*" kept running through my mind. I closed my eyes and concentrated on John's kiss.

When we broke, I noticed the stars were beginning to fade. I ran a hand over John's biceps. It felt firm and smooth. Probably all those sun salutations. "Why yoga?"

John lay back and stared up into the sky, his profile clearly visible in the growing light. "I got into it in college. I liked the discipline. I was an earnest young man, very serious about my studies, and yoga helped me manage the stress.

It was frowned on in seminary, so I stopped. That first year after I left the priesthood was rough. I was thirty-five and had nothing, no money, and no marketable skills. Paul stayed on in Minnesota to finish his contract. I moved to Chicago, where an ex-priest runs a sort of halfway house for people leaving religious orders. I got a job at a fast-food restaurant. Yoga provided structure to my days, and eventually I got my certification."

I thought about my own professional fall. Papa had been there to pick me up. "What about your family. Couldn't they help out?"

John's hand jerked in mine, but his voice was calm. "No. It was hard on them. They were proud to have a priest for a son. I came out to them the week before I officially left the priesthood. Suffice it to say that that visit didn't go well." He shrugged. "But everything worked out okay. The organization in Chicago found me this job, and we moved down here. Paul was very excited about the prospect of taking over the resort when Karina retired, but obviously that didn't pan out."

"But—"

"Shhh. Listen."

It started as a few chirps here and there, and built. I lay on the blanket as the jungle around us erupted in birdsong. The light grew, and I could make out birds in the trees surrounding us—birds flew over us, splashed in the river, cawed at each other, swooped down for food, burst from bushes in great clouds of color. The sound swelled like a symphony coming to crescendo and then settled as other sounds intruded—music from a radio, conversation from a nearby house, the *click* and *clop* of hooves on the trail.

I smiled at John as we stood and folded the blanket. "That was beautiful. Thank you."

He nodded. "I thought you'd like it."

The walk home was easier in the light. The tourists weren't up yet. The people we passed were friendly in an on-my-way-to-work kind of way, and I missed the warmth of John's hand in mine.

Chapter Seventeen

Karina arrived on Sunday at noon surrounded by a crowd of people who *oohed* and *aahed* over the lunch I laid out for them. Over the next few days, I adjusted to a new rhythm. I was up at dawn making breakfast, which slid into a continuous flow of lunch, afternoon snacks, dinner, and dessert. I took my time with the food, reveling in the chance to deliver meals that satisfied both the eye and the palate. After a month in a windowless tin box, slopping food onto platters for someone else to decorate, assembling beautiful plates in an open kitchen with a view of the ocean felt like the first long, deep breaths of summer. The people were pleasant and seemed pleased with the food. Once I got the hang of it, I never felt slammed but always stayed busy. The best part was, at the end of each day, I fell into John's bed.

Over the course of the week, I learned the idiosyncrasies of my new kitchen, the names of all the guests, the fastest routes around the resort and into town, and got to know the family who ran the local grocery well enough to be able to call down for last-minutes supplies—a few of which they actually had in stock. I found time for a run each day. That let me explore some of the area trails. At night I studied the planes of John's body, the spot on his neck that made him stop whatever else he was doing when I kissed it, the way his skin tasted on a hot night, the exact pressure of my teeth on his nipple that made him groan.

On Friday I packed sack lunches, and we walked the group down to the docks where they hopped on local fishermen's boats for a whale-watching expedition. John and I caught the Puerto Vallarta boat and spent the day food shopping, arriving back in time for me to prepare a farewell feast. On Saturday morning I was amazed as three different guests took me aside after breakfast and pressed folded bills into my hand. The tips doubled my salary for the week.

Karina left with the group on the eleven o'clock boat, saying she'd be back for lunch the next day, this time with a therapeutic writing group. Whatever that was, it would translate to seventeen hungry people for me to feed. John found me in the kitchen, organizing shelves in preparation for the next onslaught.

I leaned into his kiss. "You do know that Maria and her cleaning crew are still here."

He shook his head. "Her mother isn't well today. She said she'll send her niece up early tomorrow morning to finish up."

"We're alone?"

"Uh-huh." He tongued the crazy-making spot on my earlobe.

I ran my hand down his back to fondle his ass through his thin cotton pants.

He pulled back and looked into my eyes. "You told me that I needed to get to know you through your food. Well, I want to show you my yoga in return. We've talked so much about who I was when I was a priest. Let me show you who I am now. Come over to the studio and watch me practice."

I nodded and followed him out of the kitchen, grabbing a bottle of cooking oil on the way out, just in case.

The yoga studio was actually a large, open, tiled patio. The view of the ocean, river, and opposite hillside was spectacular. John piled mats and bolsters into a makeshift chair for me.

He laid down a dark blue mat, pulled his shirt over his head, and dropped it to the patio floor. "The asanas—poses—are only one of the limbs of yoga. We do them to enhance our ability to sit in meditation, to bring ourselves closer to the Divine. Which is not such a strange thing for an ex-priest to do."

I swallowed hard as my cock noticed how hot he looked. "You teach half-naked?"

"No. But I want you to really see me." He stepped to the front of his mat and inhaled deeply. I'd taken a yoga class when I was new in recovery. Didn't much like it, but I thought I knew what to expect as he raised his arms up over his head and did a swan dive forward on the exhale. But I'd never seen anything as beautiful as John moving through the poses. His muscles bulged and elongated under his skin. He held himself an inch from the floor, only his toes and fingers touching, his arms at perfect right angles. When he swung forward, his body formed a lovely arc, from the tops of his toes to the wild tangle of his hair. On the next breath, he shifted back to make a triangle of his body.

He continued, his movements like a long, fluid dance. More than sexy, it was mesmerizing, and I found myself matching my breath to his. He made poses I would have thought impossible look easy, and I was blown away by his strength and grace. When he finished, I was speechless and incredibly turned on.

John's normal social awkwardness returned, and he stood watching me, chewing on his bottom lip.

I realized I'd been holding my breath and let it out slowly. "You're amazing," I whispered.

He squatted in front of me. "You liked it?"

I leaned into him and ran my hand down his chest, lingering at his waistband. "It was the most beautiful thing I've ever seen."

His gaze met mine and traveled to the bulge in my pants. Tipping forward, he pinned me to the pile of mats with his knees and cradled my head in his hands, pulling me into a deep, hungry kiss. My tongue met his as I carried him down on top of me. I traced the muscles of his back, feeling them moving under my hands. His skin was like silk.

It felt completely transgressive to make love on an open patio where anyone might stumble upon us, but I didn't care. I wanted to feel him against me. I was as hard as the tile beneath us. I didn't care how we did it, but I needed it to happen right now.

I fumbled with the drawstring of his pants. He stood up and pulled them off. I squirmed out of my own clothes, not taking my eyes off his long, lean body, silhouetted against the view. His cock, which had stayed calm throughout his yoga practice, was standing out straight. I rolled to the side and reached for the cooking oil.

John dropped to his knees beside me and caught my arm. He looked intently into my eyes. "I want you to…to do it to me."

I ran my thumb over his jaw, feeling the scratch of his stubble. "Are you sure? I mean, we're fine the way we are. I like it, actually."

His face softened, and he slid down beside me so that our whole bodies touched. "I like it too. But today I want to feel what you feel, to know what it has been like for you."

The look he gave me was so tender I was afraid I'd say something stupid. Instead I pulled his face down to mine and kissed him as hard and as long and as deeply as I could.

We broke, and he rolled away from me, pressing his ass against me. I dribbled cooking oil onto my fingers and gently touched his asshole. He jumped.

I leaned to kiss his shoulder and whisper into his ear. "We'll take our time, honey. There's no rush."

I let my finger circle slowly until I saw the muscles of his shoulders relax. After slicking my other hand with more cooking oil, I reached around to fist his cock at the same moment I slid the tip of my finger inside him. He gasped and thrust into my hand and back onto my finger. I kept kissing his shoulder and murmuring his name, telling him how hot he was, how much I wanted him. All the while I tightened my hand against his cock and opened him slowly with my fingers. Counting tiles in the patio to keep myself from going over, I brought John to the edge of orgasm and backed off and did it again and backed off until I was three-finger fucking him and he was begging for me.

I slathered so much oil on my dick that my whole pelvis dripped grease. I meant to push in the tip and let him adjust, but once my cock hit that hot, tight ass, I couldn't hold myself back any longer, and I buried myself in him. His ass tightened around me for a moment. He took a deep breath, let it out, and relaxed.

"I'm not going to last long," I whispered, moving as slowly as I could, trying to find the spot.

"Oh, David." John's breath caught. I'd found it, and I let myself start pounding. John's cock slid through my hand. He hauled me into a kiss. His whole body began to tremble, and I stroked harder, fucked harder, kissed harder. His ass clenched around me. I felt the pulse of his cock in my hand. I quit counting tiles and let myself go. With each thrust I felt like I was climbing inside him, like our skin was dissolving, the barriers between us gone, and I was falling into him, fusing with him, gasping his name over and over like a mantra as I flowed into him in body-wracking pulses that seemed to go on and on and on.

John grabbed my arm and held me close as our heartbeats gradually slowed. Eventually he let go and pulled away with a pop and a wince.

He rolled to face me. "That was…"

"Are you okay?" I asked.

He nodded. "Astonishingly vulnerable. That's how it makes me feel. Is it like that for you?"

I brushed a lock of hair off his face. "Something like that."

He closed his eyes. "There's too much love in that for it to be a sin."

Love. I let the word bounce around my head, wrapped my arms around him, and sank onto the mat. I was almost asleep before I heard him get up and move away.

***

And so it continued for the next two months. From Sunday to Saturday we were surrounded by people. John taught his yoga, and I fed the masses. At some point each week, we went to Puerto Vallarta to shop, and I caught a meeting while John went to Mass. Saturday night we frolicked naked through La Serenidad. Sunday morning it started all over again, with new names to learn and food allergies to accommodate.

The weather got warmer. I packed away my chef's pants and cooked in shorts. The guests wore less and less as they wandered the common rooms. John packed away the blankets from what I'd taken to thinking of as our bed. The final group spent most of their time at the beach.

Karina left three days after they did, and John and I were alone. The summer stretched out before us—long and hot with only a few breaks in our solitude, individual guests scheduled to come sweat for a week or so. The air got hotter and hotter.

In July, the rains came. Storms blew through, dumping torrents of water. The good news was that we could take long showers. Orchids bloomed, and in between downpours, the hummingbirds were everywhere. The bad news was we needed a shower after every time we left the house and returned covered in mud. The sheets and clothes smelled of mildew and wouldn't dry. Mosquitoes tried to empty our veins. The air was so thick it was like living in a sauna.

For months, John and I spent rainy days lying in bed, escaping the mosquitoes and watching land crabs scuttle across the floor. If it was too hot to fuck, we told each other stories of our childhoods. I talked about Antonio, about Rick, and John talked about his days as a young priest. I started to feel like I'd known him all my life. I didn't ask about Paul. I think I was afraid of what he'd say. After our morning on the sandbar, John didn't volunteer information about that time of his life—other than to say he was glad it was over.

It wasn't perfect. We rarely ate the same food, and no matter how many times I tried it, I couldn't get into doing yoga. Instead I ran in the early morning, if it was cool enough, and swam in the afternoon. We took the boat to Puerto

Vallarta every couple of weeks, and when we got there, we mostly went our separate ways.

To some degree it felt like we were old lovers, set in our routine. I knew how I felt and I hoped he did too, but he didn't say it and neither did I.

Chapter Eighteen

Rosh Hashanah and Yom Kippur fell in September—
the rainiest month yet. I made a round egg bread—a challah
that we dipped in honey for a sweet new year. John offered to
fast with me for Yom Kippur. There was a temple in Puerto
Vallarta, but instead of going, we stayed home and talked
about the things we regretted. I asked if he was sorry, either
that he joined, or left, the priesthood, and was surprised when
he answered that it was his relationship with his mother that
bothered him the most—he'd been her best dream and had
turned into her worst nightmare. Which made me remember
my own mother and to be grateful she lived long enough to
see me sober. We broke our fast with a Jewish-Mexican feast of
chopped liver, tamales, and papayas.

The last morning of September dawned clear and
relatively cool. When I got out of bed, John was nowhere in
sight, and I assumed he'd gone down to the yoga studio for
his morning practice. I pulled on loose shorts, laced up my
running shoes, tied a bandanna around my head to keep the
sweat out of my eyes, and took off down the hill and on to the

upriver trail. By now most people knew me enough to wish me good morning as I trotted past. Once the pavement ended and my feet hit the dirt path, I pumped it up. It felt good to push myself hard. A shift was coming. The summer was ending. Karina would be back in a week, and soon the cocoon we'd been living in would burst open.

Birds called on both sides of the path. The air smelled sweet from wet vegetation. Everywhere flowers bloomed, and leaves shone vibrant green. The rains had saturated the earth for four months, and the land had come alive. When I turned around to head home, a flash of color caught my eye. A flock of military macaws—the classic, pirate parrots—flew over, their green, yellow, and blue plumage like a blessing.

I was dripping sweat when I stepped through the front entryway of La Serenidad. John sat at one of the tables, talking with a handsome blond. They looked up. Something I couldn't read flitted across John's face.

"Hey." I stopped a few feet from the table, thinking that any closer and they'd be overwhelmed by my sweaty stink.

John's smile was sad. "Good morning. David, this is my old friend Paul."

I blinked and looked at the man more closely. "Paul." The man John had left the priesthood for. The one Frank said he loved more than God.

Paul stood. He was easily five inches taller than me, broad-shouldered and movie-star handsome. He held out his hand. "David, I've heard so much about you. It's good to finally meet."

Heard so much about me? I looked at John, who was staring distractedly at the table. I stepped forward and shook Paul's hand. His grip was firm and his smile controlled. His gaze slid over my bare chest like a snake. I pulled back, made my excuses, and headed toward the shower.

I stood under the spray, trying to make sense of the whole interaction. What was Paul doing here? And had John been in contact with him all along? *"I've heard so much about you."* When? How? And again, what was he doing here? And how did John feel about it all?

I couldn't come up with answers, so I turned off the water, dried myself, and pulled on fresh clothes. I stood looking in the mirror, comparing myself to the Aryan dream I'd just met. I hadn't expected Paul to be so flat-out gorgeous. No wonder John left God for him. I paused again at the bathroom door. I had no idea what I was supposed to do next. Join them? Leave them alone? Cook? What was Paul doing here anyway?

It turned out not to matter. When I entered the dining room, it was empty. I looked up toward John's hut and didn't see anyone. I spotted a note on the kitchen counter. *David, I've taken Paul to visit Maria. Back soon.*

Maria lived down the hill and across the river. They'd be gone at least an hour, maybe more. I stood for a long time, trying to decide what to do. The only thing I could think of was to work, so I went into the kitchen to start the inventory I'd been putting off all summer. Counting canned goods sounded like a reasonable way to keep myself from wondering what Paul wanted and why he'd come visiting John to find it. John could tell me himself when they returned from Maria's.

If Paul wanted him back, what would John do? I knew he cared for me. But he loved Paul more than God. That's hard competition.

Worrying about it didn't help. I got a pad and listed what we had, noted what we needed, and reorganized the cookware, cutlery, and flatware. I checked the cloth napkins for spots, cleaned both refrigerators, and scrubbed the counters. After sharpening all my knives, I turned on Karina's computer. I updated the Web page, checked reservations, answered an e-mail from Karina, and another from my father. *Everything is fine. It's all good. Don't worry about us down here.* Karina wanted to know if I'd made up my mind about the next season. I checked the time on her e-mail. If I'd answered her right when she'd sent it, I would have said yes, absolutely, I've never been happier, sign me up for the rest of my life. I wrote that we'd talk when she arrived. If John left with Paul, I'd have to think hard about whether I could stay.

The sky darkened. I could see the storm coming from a long way away. I shut down the computer and sat in a wicker chair to watch the rain sweep across the ocean, drench the beach, and climb the mountains, until a thick sheet of water obscured the view. The sound on the roof was like snare drums. The room had gotten so dark it felt like night. I had nothing to do but watch the rain and wonder what was happening to my life.

The afternoon graded into evening, and they didn't come home. The rain continued relentlessly, dumping torrents of water on mountain, river, and sea. I wondered if maybe I'd missed them, if they were up in John's hut. The hill was slick with mud. I had to crawl on hands and knees to get up to there. It was empty. I lit the glass-chimney candle to make sure John's things were still there. In the flickering candlelight, I couldn't see anything missing. When I turned to go, the glass cylinder slipped from my hand and shattered on the floor. The naked candle hissed and went out. I stood in the dark, surrounded by unseen broken glass, and remembered the taste of good whiskey.

A drink wouldn't make it better.

I didn't want John, or even Paul, to walk barefoot across broken glass. Unless I wanted to stay crouched on the floor until dawn, I didn't have much choice. I did what I could to sweep the glass to one side, using my T-shirt to shield my hands from the worst of it. I walked back into the storm and slid most of the way downhill to the main lodge. I used the hand pump in the washhouse to fill a bucket with water, propped a flashlight against the wall, and sat on the floor of the shower for a long time, picking tiny slivers from my feet and hands.

Later, my wounds wrapped in bandages and antiseptic, I paced the kitchen, listening to the crickets, the rain, and in the distance, the rhythmic slap of the waves. The cuts on my feet stung with each step.

Why weren't they back, and why hadn't John called? John was somewhere with Paul. That stupid phrase of Frank's kept running around my head.

The rain on the roof was deafening. I wanted a drink so badly my head hurt. I picked up the phone to call Ty. It was dead. I clicked the button over and over again. Nothing. It explained why John hadn't called. What would he do if he couldn't get ahold of me? Would he brave the storm and come home? I had a sudden image of John trying to cross the swollen river.

Panic coursed through me. The images from my dreams of John emerging from the ocean crashed against other images of John being swallowed by a torrent of water. All those dreams had held danger from deadly spiders and snakes. I thought John was the antidote, but maybe it had been a sign.

I was finally, truly, in love again, and I couldn't take it if he died, too.

I slipped my running shoes over my bandaged feet and ran out into the storm. Rain slapped my face. The path down the mountain was slick with mud. I slid and fell, stood and stumbled down the trail through the dark. The jagged end of a broken branch tore my shirt and gouged my side. I cursed and kept moving.

The waterfall roared. The pool around it had overflowed, and I slipped on the slick rock walkway, catching myself and yelling as my cut hands hit the pavement. I got up and started down the path toward the river. I didn't know what I'd do when I got there, but I felt drawn by images of John not coming out of the water but being drawn into it, taken under, and washed away.

The path ended where it was engulfed by the swollen river. I waded ankle deep into the water. On a calm day at low tide, people waded across easily. Now the storm and tide had conspired to create a raging torrent that pulled against my leg as I stood squinting into the rain. Wind and water slammed against me. Logs and weeds tumbled by, and I felt foolish for standing there waiting for John when he was probably safe and dry, sipping hot tea in Maria's tidy house. I turned to go back home and saw him, a hundred yards upriver. He was waist deep in the water, wading across the river. From the way his arms pumped, it looked like the current was strong. He saw me and waved.

A long, dark shape barreled through the water upstream of him. I started running, gesturing wildly, splashing through the river toward John. He was looking at me. Not at the log rushing toward him. I neared, and he held out his arms, reaching for my hand. I screamed as the wood hit him in the back.

His head disappeared beneath the water. The log rushed past me. I felt like I was moving in slow motion, slogging through the water toward where he had been. When I got there, I stopped and scanned the river downstream. Hoping. Praying. Calling his name.

Something pale was caught in the eddy behind a sandbank. I stumbled toward it, the river helping now as the current pushed me downstream. John's white shirt drew me like a beacon. The river smashed me into him. I grabbed him under the armpits and pulled. He was a limp weight in my arms as I dragged him up onto the sandbar. He looked still and pale, like a statue. Pressing myself against his back, I rolled him onto his side, trying to remember what I was supposed to do next. Mouth-to-mouth? Heimlich? CPR? I pounded his back.

After what felt like forever, John's head jerked, and he started coughing and gasping. My tears mixed with the rain as I held him and he vomited water. Eventually the sputtering and gasping stopped, and John breathed beside me.

He rested his head against mine. "I think you saved my life."

"Or endangered it. You might have seen the log if I hadn't distracted you."

He ran a hand along his back and winced. "Was that what hit me? I think it knocked the wind out of me. Next thing I knew, I was sucking water."

The rain slowed.

"Do you think you can walk?"

He looked across the river. "I don't want to stay here, so I better try."

"Okay?" We stood. I wrapped my arm around his back.

He took a deep breath and winced. "Let's do it."

The current pushed against us, and the sand slipped beneath my feet. But with John's arm across my shoulder, it felt like I could do anything. By the time we got across to the bank, the rain had stopped. We climbed slowly back home to La Casa de la Serenidad.

***

We carried candles to the shower room. John set them around the room while I pumped water. As we peeled off our wet clothes, John touched the ragged edge of a bandage hanging off my hand. "What's this?"

I looked down, surprised it was still there. "I went looking for you and ended up breaking the glass chimney over your candle. I'll replace it as soon as I can get to Puerto Vallarta."

He grabbed my hand and brought it close to his face. His voice was tight as he asked, "Are you hurt?"

I laughed. "It's been a rough night all around, but I'll live."

We stood in the shower for a long time, scrubbing the sand and dirt from each other's wounds by candlelight. John had a bruise forming on his back and a gash on one leg. In addition to the cuts on my hands and feet, I had scraped knees and a cut on my side. I made a mental note to add bandages to the list of things we'd need in Puerto Vallarta since the night's drama had depleted our supplies.

We collapsed together on the single bed off the kitchen. John laid his head on my shoulder. "It was foolish of me to try to cross the river. But I was afraid you were worried."

I stroked his wet hair. "I was."

John caressed my chest. "I'm sorry. Paul wanted to visit Maria and her family. He was close to them while he was here. The storm came, and the phones went out. I left Paul at Maria's. They thought I was insane, but I couldn't wait until daylight."

I kissed his temple. "I was going crazy up here with jealousy."

"Why?" He twisted his head to look at me.

"Paul." I held my breath.

John's brow wrinkled. "You don't need to worry about Paul. I gave him what he wanted. He'll go home on the afternoon boat tomorrow."

I could barely see his eyes in the dark. "I thought you were what he wanted."

He snorted. "Hardly."

"What, then? It's a long way to come to visit Maria and her family."

John sighed. After a moment, he spoke. "Paul's getting married. To a woman. He brought an affidavit for me to sign, testifying that we'd never engaged in sodomy. Evidently that fine point is as important to his bride as it was to him."

"What? That's revolting." I gaped at him. "Did you sign it?"

I felt him shrug. "Why not? It's true."

"Oh, honey, I'm so sorry." I rested my cheek against his forehead. "That must hurt."

He kissed my chin and whispered, "I think he's a fool."

I pulled back, angry at Paul for him. "But he was the love of your life. The man you left God for, the one you loved more than God."

John laughed. "You think I abandoned God for *Paul?* That I love Paul more than God? How'd you get that?"

I felt myself blushing. It was a good thing it was dark. "Frank said—"

"Frank's a sentimental idiot." There was humor in his voice. "How can anyone leave God? That's like leaving your breath behind. As for loving Paul more than God, that's absurd. I didn't leave God. I left the priesthood. Mind you, that was a very hard thing to do, and Paul helped me go, for which I'll be forever grateful. But that's it."

I looked at the ceiling. "If he had come back for you, would you have gone?"

John wrapped his leg around mine and nestled closer. He shook his head. "No. I'm happy right where I am."

***

At dawn we carried a mop and bucket up the hill. John moved stiffly, and I limped behind. The path was still slippery with mud, and there were gouges in the dirt beside the path that were shaped like my elbows and knees. John didn't say anything but kept glancing back at me with concern.

"It was a stupid system anyway." John tossed the last of the big pieces of glass into a paper bag. "It was only a matter of time before the wind or some animal knocked it down."

"I'll replace it," I muttered, edging the broom along the floor where it met the wall.

He squatted with the dustpan. "Don't bother. We have flashlights."

We swept and mopped and, between us, got up even the smallest shards of glass.

I dumped the dirty water in the old outhouse behind the hut. When I came back to the room, John was staring out at the ocean. He sat down on the rock wall and gestured for me to join him.

I swung one leg over and leaned against a pillar, facing him. John scooted so he could rest his back against the next pillar and stretched his legs out in front. With the two of us framing a view of ocean and jungle, it would have made a lovely photo.

John folded his hands on his lap, closed his eyes, and started to talk. "I struggled with my sexuality for a long time, but by the time I met Paul, I knew that the God I believed in had made me who I am and that if it was okay with him, it should be okay with me." He opened his eyes and looked at me. I nodded. He continued, still watching me, "I was thirty-five when I met Paul. I'm forty-one now."

He paused.

I said, "Thirty-four. And I don't have a problem with our age difference."

He inclined his head. "Paul was twenty-three, fresh out of college. He was far too young, and I was much too flattered. Pride. It trips me up every time. The whole experience of leaving the priesthood and encountering physical love for the first time was overwhelming, and it wasn't until we moved down here that I saw how unsuited we were. By then, it was too late."

John picked a bougainvillea flower from a nearby bush. He watched it twirl in his fingers. "It's something I'd been hearing from parishioners for years—how lonely you could be in a relationship. Paul wrestled with his homosexuality. I tried to help and ended up feeling more like his priest than his lover. In the end"—John shrugged—"it wasn't enough for either of us. It was a relief when he left."

"I think I know what you mean." I leaned back against the pillar. "My breakup with Rick was financially disastrous, but I didn't miss him, and it made me realize I'd been on autopilot for a long time."

John's gaze was earnest. "After Paul left, every morning I prayed to meet someone stronger, more mature, someone who knew what it was like to have to give up everything and start again. You're the answer to those prayers."

A shiver ran through me. "I dreamed about you. Back in Portland, before we met. Until last night I kept telling myself I'd made you fit the dream, not the other way around, but it was you. My merman. Only I had the dream all wrong."

As I told him about the snakes and spiders and how he'd looked exactly as I'd dreamed him right before the log slammed into him the night before, John's eyes widened. He took a deep breath. "Soon Karina is going to ask whether you'll stay. What'll you tell her?"

"After all that, the prayers and the dream, you have to ask? It's like God brought us together." I looked out at the view. "It'll be hard, of course, living in paradise with you, but I'll manage."

I stood and held out my hand. John took it and let me lead him to the bed. We dropped our clothes like the accustomed lovers we were. I looked at the bruises mottling John's skin and was overwhelmed with gratitude to have him still alive and beautiful in front of me. We slipped under the mosquito netting. The bed swung beneath us as we tumbled together. John's leg fell in between mine, and I kissed him, sliding my tongue deep into his mouth, and cradling his ass in my hands.

When we broke, I stared into John's gorgeous green eyes and whispered, "Paul will be here soon. I know it's petty, but when I see him next, I want to be feeling your cum dripping out of me."

John groaned, and his cock hardened against my hip. He kissed me again, and my body came to life.

"We don't have much time," John murmured into my mouth.

I reached over my head to the pocket John had sewn in the mosquito netting to hold the lube. "I'm not in the mood for slow." I slicked his cock, which was already rock hard. "Although I'm in favor of sodomy. It would be okay with me if he caught us with your cock in my ass." I threw my legs over John's shoulders.

"Oh." It came out as a puff of air. John gripped the cheeks of my ass. I guided his cock into place and held his gaze as he pushed in. I felt naked in a new way, like I was letting him into my soul.

I grabbed his ass and thrust back into him. "Please, fuck me."

The look on John's face went from tender to white-hot. He held my ass and shifted to his knees, his cock moving faster and faster. When he hit me right, I gasped, and he stayed there, pounding into me. I held on to his back with my calves, arched, and thrust. I grabbed my cock and started stroking in rhythm with John's cock in my ass. His gaze flew from my face to my cock. His mouth fell open, and his breath came in gasps. Words tumbled out of me as I begged him to fuck me harder, faster. I was calling out his name between gulps of air. Sweat beaded on John's forehead and chest. He looked flushed and beautiful, a fierce angel.

He gasped. "I'm…"

And I was coming so hard my toes curled, my ass cramped, and I called out, "I love you!"

John fell on top of me and stayed there, covering my face and neck and chest with fluttery kisses. He rolled to the side, pulled me close, and fell asleep. I watched the rise and fall of his chest. I might scream it, but for John, falling asleep beside me was his own quiet declaration of love.

***

I woke to see Paul standing in the entryway, staring at us. Our eyes met. He turned and left. I listened to his footsteps until they were covered by the sound of the breeze, the trees, and the ocean in the distance. My jealous fit seemed distant, and I felt incredibly sad for Paul. He'd chosen a hard path.

I shook John awake. "Get dressed. It's time to say good-bye to Paul."

He rolled onto his back and smiled at me. "Why don't you make us all one of your spectacular breakfasts?"

I owed Paul a lot. Without him, John might never have left the priesthood. Breakfast was the very least I could give him in return.

Chapter Nineteen

The fourth night of Hanukkah fell on a Saturday. John and I had the place to ourselves. I took my menorah down to the dining hall and set it on the edge of the floor, where the candles would be visible across the jungle. John and I sat with our legs dangling over the edge as we watched the sunset. When the last rays were down and the horizon rimmed with pink, I said the blessing and lit the candles.

We watched in silence as the candles burned.

John's profile was as familiar in the dark as the hand I reached to grasp. "The two biggest events of my life happened during Hanukkah."

He turned to look at me, the candlelight reflected in his eyes.

"It was the fifth night when Antonio died. And ten years later, I lit the first night candles before going to the bar to meet you." I squeezed his hand, then dropped it as I stood up. "I got you a present."

I trotted back to the little room off the kitchen that I used as a storage closet and dug the cardboard box from under the bed. Some animal had chewed a corner of the wrapping, but what could I expect living in the middle of a jungle?

I sat down next to John and handed it to him.

He turned it around in his hands several times. "I've never had a Hanukkah present before."

He unwrapped it slowly, pausing to neatly fold the chewed wrapping paper. He opened the box and pulled out the square, stained-glass lantern I'd commissioned from a Puerto Vallartan artist.

"Here, let me light it so you can see." I pulled matches from my pocket, unlatched one side of the box, and opened it up. John held the lantern while I lit the candle inside and closed the latch.

"This is beautiful," he whispered, turning it to see each side.

"It's us. There's the cross, a Star of David, an om symbol, and a pink triangle on the side that opens to remind us of what we share." I pointed toward the hook in the top. "We can hang it from the ceiling so wind or animals or jealous lovers can't knock it over."

"I love it." John held it by the hook, wrapped his hand around the back of my neck, and kissed me softly, his lips brushing mine. "I have something for you too. It's a Christmas present, but I don't see why I can't give it to you early."

"You don't have to—"

But he was already on his feet and striding toward the door. "I'll be right back."

I watched the Hanukkah candles sputter out. Patches of flickering light from the new lamp painted our symbols on the tile in red, blue, purple, and pink. I passed my hands through the light, letting the colors drift across my skin and decorate me with our separate and shared beliefs, and feeling how we meshed, John in me and me in him.

John slid down beside me. He handed me a small black jewelry box.

I looked at him. "You—"

"Open it." He rested his hand on my back.

Inside was a silver medallion on a long black cord. I held it close to the lantern to see. On one side of the medallion was a line drawing etched in black with two entwined male figures. I turned it over and read, *1 Samuel 18:1.*

I looked at John. "It's beautiful. But I haven't studied the Bible since my bar mitzvah. First Samuel is in my part of the Bible, right?"

A quiet laugh rumbled in John's chest. "I believe the interdenominationally correct way to refer to it is as the Hebrew Bible, but yes, that's where it is."

I looked down at the engraving. "What does it say?"

John leaned into me, his breath warm on my cheek. "'The soul of Jonathan was knit with the soul of David, and Jonathan loved him as his own soul.'"

I stared at him. "That's in the Bible?"

"Read it. It's quite a love story." He kissed my neck. "I'm a conventional man. You know how uncomfortable I am with the idea of casual relationships."

I laughed. "I'm glad you don't have to run away anymore."

He caressed my head. "I would have had the verse engraved on the inside of a ring, but I thought this wouldn't get in your way in the kitchen. I mean it as that kind of pledge between us, though. Will you accept?"

I held it out to him. "If you'll put it on me."

John's fingers trembled a little as he slipped the pendant over my head. His lips barely moved as he whispered, "What God has brought together, let no man put asunder." He stared at the spot over my heart where the medallion fell.

"Is this the part where we kiss?"

His lips were soft and tasted like hope. I held his hand over the silver disk and let myself believe.

The End

Dev Bentham

Dev Bentham writes soulful m/m romance. Her characters are flawed and damaged adult men who may not even know what they are missing, but whose lives are transformed by true love.

Love is a Light Titles by Dev Bentham

August Ice

* * * *

The TARNISHED SOULS Series
Learning from Isaac
Fields of Gold
Sacred Hearts

Coming soon to Love is a Light:
Bread, Salt and Wine

Other books by Dev
Driving into the Sun
Nobody's Home
Painting in the Rain
Moving in Rhythm

love is a Light

Tarnished Souls 4:
Bread, Salt and Wine

Coming Spring 2015 from Love is a Light

by Dev Bentham

2005: An April Wedding

The band was too loud, the bride looked like a skeleton, and I had a raging headache. What a way to spend Friday night. I kept trying to remember why working for a prestigious LA restaurant had seemed like a better deal than my comfortable line job at a respectable place in New York. Especially since this particular gig had required supervising the creation of hundreds of puffy cheese minisoufflés, artichoke and bacon rolls, and duck liver wraps, all of which had to be carted from the L'Ouest kitchens to this golf-course-sized Beverley Hills backyard, where a chubby record company executive was marrying Madam Skeletor in lavish style.

It wasn't the menu I would have suggested for this fat-conscious crowd, but until I could convince my boss to offer less pretentious and difficult-to-serve food, I'd be stuck with whatever he arranged. And unpretentious wasn't of particular value to Stephan—that's pronounced "Stefaaan"—Becker.

Any sane chef would design a separate menu for catering, featuring finger food, fresh fruits, and meals that could be plated with grace. I looked at the tiny bites of rich food starting to congeal in the warming trays and considered whether it was time to bring a new batch from the van.

A silver platter appeared at my left elbow, and a voice suggested, "I can start offering those to the guests so you can freshen up this station."

I turned, and there he was. A few inches shorter than me, with spiky blond hair and a big smile, he wore the standard waiter's uniform of black pants and a black button-down shirt. He managed to look like he'd just stepped off the runway during New York's fashion week.

He held out the tray. "You're Mr. Zajac, the new catering chef, right? I'm Kenny Marks, waiter extraordinaire." He had an exuberant lilt to his voice. "And I'd love to help you get rid of that food."

I could use a friend on staff. "Call me George. You seem to know your way around. Have you worked for L'Ouest long?"

He held the platter while I arranged the food. "I was with the company for the first event, a horrid little birthday party." He shuddered dramatically. "The wife had decorated the whole house in black for the poor man's fortieth. It was brutal."

"This is my first job catering." I nodded toward the crowd. "Any advice you have for me would be appreciated."

Kenny looked out at the gathering. "You see that guy in the maroon bow tie? He's the groom's financial manager. Make sure he's happy. That's where your check and your tip are coming from. And over there's the bride's mother. Rumor is that back home in Dallas she hosts soirees on a regular basis. She and the daughter are supposed to be close. You might give the mama some personal attention—people like to meet the chef, makes them feel special. The new couple is bound to entertain, and I doubt our blushing bride cooks. She'll ask mummy for advice on catering. Tips are always bigger from repeat customers."

I stared at him. "How do you know all this?"

He hefted the now full platter to his shoulder. "I keep my eyes and ears open. Here comes Libby Spencer. She's the most sought-after wedding planner in the city. Be very, very nice to her."

With that he strolled off, walking with shoulders back and a slight sway to his hips, his pants pleasingly tight across a very nice ass. What would it be like to feel that comfortable with one's sexuality? The question made me break into a sweat.

I turned my attention to Ms. Spencer. Striding toward me, tall, thin, with four-inch spiked heels that clicked on the stone pavement, she looked as formidable as any corporate attorney I'd known back in the day.

I smiled and stepped forward.

She thrust out her hand. "Libby Spencer. Call me Libby. You're the new catering chef. George, is it? I hope you're better than the little weasel L'Ouest had before. For some reason my customers like to hire your company. Mostly for the name, I think. This"—she gestured at the food—"wouldn't be my first choice of event food, but c'est la vie."

I nodded. "Perhaps we could adjust the menu."

She snorted. "Not likely, not with your prig of a chef. Never mind. You'll find I'm easy to work with as long as things go smoothly."

From a distance, I could see Skeletor gesturing toward us. Libby plastered on a brilliant smile. Out of the corner of her mouth she muttered, "This job has plenty of headaches. Don't be one of them." With that, she was gone.

I signaled one of the other waiters to replenish the warming trays. When I had everything looking good, I left an assistant in charge of the buffet and went in search of the mother of the bride. It wouldn't hurt to spread a little charm.

Kenny beamed at me from across the room. He really had a great smile.

* * *

It was after midnight by the time we got everything cleaned up and stowed away back at the restaurant. I got change for the five one-hundred-dollar bills the financial manager had pressed into my palm as we left, and doled out fifty dollars to each of the four waiters, the busboy/dishwasher, and the bartender. I stuffed one into my pocket and the others into an envelope to give the kitchen crew.

The group started toward the staff locker room, and the kitchen emptied out. Except the cute one, Kenny.

He waved his money at me. "And the momma? Was she pleased?"

I shrugged. "She says she'll call if she needs catering. We'll see." He watched me expectantly until I added, "Thanks for pointing her out."

"No problem. Glad to be of service." He shifted his weight onto one hip and looked at me from under his eyelashes. "Chef sometimes forgets to schedule me. Maybe you could put in a good word."

I nodded. He smiled and turned to leave, throwing a "good night" over his shoulder as he sauntered out the door. I stayed behind to check on the preparations for the next event, Sunday brunch for a hundred. I reviewed the work schedule and was surprised by the pang of disappointment I felt when Kenny Marks's name wasn't on the list.

By the time I made it back to the staff locker room, everyone was gone. I tossed my white coat and hat into the laundry bin and gathered my jacket and helmet. Outside, my motorcycle started immediately, and I pulled out into the warm California night.

The breeze was cool, and the thrum of the engine under my thighs gave me a feeling of power and grace. Traffic was light, and my tiredness started to melt as I sped through quiet streets. There were places I could go where people would be awake. Hot rooms with loud music and willing men. For a few minutes I let myself imagine entering the bar, scanning the crowd, and finding someone who was looking back at me with the same hunger. I shook my head. My jaw still hurt from the last overzealous cowboy I'd let ride my face. What I needed was something safer, more predictable. Not a boyfriend. I wouldn't inflict myself on anyone. But maybe I could find a regular fuck buddy who could deal with my sexual weirdness without getting too rough.

By the time I pulled into the garage, the desire for company had passed. I parked the bike and climbed the stairs to my apartment. In New York I never lived lower than the sixth floor. In Echo Park none of the apartments in my price range sat higher than the third.

The apartment building was quiet, with only the distant sounds of traffic and the pound of a rap song from somewhere down the street. I opened the door and stepped into my tiny haven. One of the many reasons I should never have married Anne was the mismatch in our living styles. Where she favored cozy contemporary, my preferred decor was stripped-down minimalism. She called it empty. I liked to think of it as sparse, monastic, Zen. For years we compromised. She decorated the apartment. I lived at the office. It was only after I moved out that I realized how hard it had been for me to breath surrounded by all that stuff. Okay, maybe decor wasn't the only reason I'd felt stifled.

I'd liked the simplicity of the second-floor studio the first time I saw it. Essentially one large room, it had a rudimentary kitchen along one wall, and windows and the doorway to the balcony along another. I'd furnished it with a big bed, a low bureau, and plenty of space. The only other furniture was the wrought-iron table and two chairs that filled the small balcony. I crossed to the kitchen and poured myself a glass of Australian chardonnay, crisp with vanilla and apple notes, and at less than ten bucks a bottle, an unsung bargain. I slid open the balcony door and sat to watch the city sleep.

I grew up miserable in the middle of cornfields. I'd felt so fucking isolated. I vowed that as soon as I could escape, I'd live in places where there'd always be someone who could hear me if I screamed. It soothed me to watch people and cars moving along crowded streets. I sipped my wine and relished watching the lights of cars. It had taken a long time for me to get there, safe, single, and unknown. So what if I was lonely? Everything had its price.

* * *

I fell asleep thinking of the way Kenny's pants hugged the curve of his ass.

And woke shaking from a dream so real I could hear the animals breathing, smell the warm mix of hay and cow combined with a pungent tang of fresh manure. I lay staring into the darkness, listening to the pound of my heart and the memory of my father's voice, alternating between whispering love and shouting the condemnation of God and all his angels.

"Pray, boy."

I was twelve again, naked and shamed, fighting not to cry as my father's belt bit into my flesh and his words seared themselves into my heart.

"Pray."

I slid from the bed onto my knees and pressed my hands together hard, imitating prayer to a God I no longer believed in, holding the position until my knees ached and the muscles in my shoulders burned. It was the only way to make the dream recede. If there was a God, he wasn't fooled by my fakery, but my subconscious was, and eventually I crawled back in bed and drifted toward sleep.

My father couldn't whip my abomination away, but some wounds never heal, and it was folly for me to believe I'd ever be fit for anything other than a quick, hard fuck in a dark alley.

* * *

I woke early, still edgy from my dream. Sun streaked in the studio window, making the floors shine. I was a sporadic exerciser at best. Back in New York I would have taken the elevator down to the basement to work out in a dark room that smelled like gym socks. In Southern California I didn't need a treadmill. I could walk along palm-tree-lined streets listening to birdsong. I rolled out of bed into old sweats and running shoes and shoved a wad of bills in my pocket.

Outside a breeze smelled of exhaust and piss. Trash blew along the curb. I started to walk quickly, plotting a path that would bring me near a bakery I'd spotted a few days before. Instead of palm-tree-lined streets, I found myself striding beside gray buildings covered with graffiti, past a drive-through dry cleaner and a mesh-fronted liquor store. I turned a corner. Ahead of me the street passed under the freeway. As I neared, I could see movement in the undergrowth behind the fence. Dozens of people moved around, rolled up bedding, chatted, and stuffed their belongings into packs, plastic bags, and shopping carts. I looked away and walked under the overpass.

I was used to seeing homeless people. The last place I lived was New York City, for God's sake. But something about watching the hillside come alive like that shook me. I kept walking until I found the bakery I'd been meaning to try. Sweet things comforted me. One of my earliest memories was of my mom handing me a cookie warm from the oven while my ass still stung from my dad's belt. No wonder I was fucked up.

The bakery smelled of yeast and caramelized sugar. I ordered coffee and a dozen doughnuts to go. On a bench outside the bakery, I sat drinking coffee and basking in the spring sun.

In front of me, a woman climbed out of a battered green sedan. She stretched and yawned before opening the back door. I saw her shake sleeping children awake. One, two, three, they piled out of the car and stood blinking beside her in pajamas, with their hair mussed and sleep lines creasing their faces. The woman shouldered a giant, brightly colored cloth bag, slung her youngest onto her hip, held the middle girl's hand, looked both ways, and crossed the street. The oldest, a boy of maybe seven, skipped ahead. I watched as they all entered a gas station. I ate a doughnut and licked the sweet stickiness from my fingers. As I pulled another from the bag, the little family emerged, looking freshly washed and neatly dressed. They crossed the street, headed for the car. The girl—who couldn't have been more than five—spotted me, or rather, my doughnut. After maybe twenty gawking seconds, she looked down at her shoes. The mom considered me. I guess I looked safe enough, because she simply nodded and opened the car door so the kids could pile in.

I looked from my bag of doughnuts and to the car full of undoubtedly hungry kids. Not that doughnuts were a nutritious breakfast. But they tasted good—soft, cakey with a hint of cinnamon. She was closing her door by the time I got there. I knocked on the window. She looked up at me with quick suspicion.

"Sorry. Didn't mean to startle you. I thought the kids might like some doughnuts." I held up the bag.

Her eyes narrowed.

I patted my belly. "If I eat any more of these, the exercise I got this morning isn't going to make any difference." She kept staring at me. I could hear rustling in the backseat, but I held her gaze and put on my best Iowa farm-boy smile. "No hidden agenda, ma'am. Just thought your kids could use these more than me." I set the bag on the roof of the car and walked away.

By the time I walked back under the overpass, the crowd of folks sleeping along the highway had scattered. A couple of men sat on the curb talking. A few more stood by the on-ramp with signs advertising that they'd work for food. An old woman shouted curses as she pushed an overflowing shopping cart along the road. I thought about sweetness. I might have had ghosts and demons banging around in my head, but at least I had a home, a job, and hope.

And I didn't need to be at work until the next morning, and I knew how to make doughnuts. When I got home, I looked up the nearest restaurant supply company, hopped on my bike, and drove off in search of a deep fat fryer. Maybe I couldn't change the world, but I might be able to make a few people's lives a little sweeter.

* * *

Less than a week passed before, as Kenny had predicted, Bride Skeletor's mother called to arrange a meeting about catering her daughter's first cocktail party. Although the party was months away and the happy couple was still on holiday, Mom was eager to make the arrangements as soon as possible. As I scheduled a consultation with her, I was amazed. I'd thought it would be ages before I had an opportunity to organize something on my own.

Chef Stephan was yelling at a young prep cook when I set down the phone. He was a small, precise man with a sharp tongue honed over thirty years in high-powered kitchens, and his style was to keep order by beating the staff into compliance. If I had been running my own kitchen, I wouldn't have chosen his particular mix of venom and haughty distance, but I'd only been in the business a few years, so what did I know?

As soon as I had him alone, I got to the point. "I'd like to develop a few dishes especially for the catering menu."

His face hardened. "What's wrong with what we offer?"

I used my calm-the-client voice, developed through years of reassuring nervous investors who had trusted me with their life savings. "Wouldn't it be better to have a few offerings suited to both our working conditions and to lighter palates?"

"No." He stood with his hands on his hips and scowled like a bulldog. "The menu will not change."

In my old life, before I became a cook, I spent a lot of time with people who were used to getting their way. I had been one of them.

I inclined my head in deference to his oh-so-muchness and asked, "Why not?"

His arm exploded out from his body as he made a sweeping gesture that encompassed the kitchen, the dining room, and the universe beyond. "Because when people contact us for catering, they expect the L'Ouest menu. They are asking to bring the restaurant into their living room. And that is what we give them."

I shook my head. "I doubt they are looking to re-create exact meals they've had here. I think they're expecting excellent food with a French twist."

"You're wrong." He waved his hand to dismiss me.

I wanted to ask, *If you don't want my input, why the fuck did you hire me?* I bit my tongue and left.

* * *

"Heard you stood up to the devil the other day." Kenny was helping me set out the artichoke salads it had taken the kitchen crew hours to plate and which would take the corporate meeting goers we were serving minutes to eat.

"If you mean Chef, it didn't do any good." I watched Kenny's hands as he placed the plates on the table. He had a knack for lining up the artichoke in perfect alignment with the knife every time. He had great hands, with elegant fingers, the masculine brush of hair at the base of each hand in sexy contrast to his manicured fingernails. I shook my head. Fantasizing about a coworker. Maybe I needed to visit the bars again after all.

Kenny was speaking. "I should have warned you. He's fanatic about the menu. If he weren't such a homophobic little twit, I'd think he had a hard-on for Louis XIV."

"He's homophobic?" I kept my voice level, trying not to betray the creep of fear Kenny's statement had triggered.

"A real prick about it. Rumor is he fired two guys for making out in the alley during break." Kenny kept talking as he placed the salads in perfect rows. "Check the schedule. Anyone he thinks is gay gets fewer shifts."

I scowled at him. The whole subject made me profoundly uncomfortable.

Kenny shrugged. "Sorry. Didn't mean to offend."

The door opened, and executives in crisp suits began filing in. From the smiles and laughter, I surmised that whatever the meeting was about, it signaled a waterfall of money. By the time I turned to Kenny to apologize for being so abrupt, he was gone. Tray in hand, he was sauntering through the crowd, handing out champagne.

I left him to it and went back to our rented kitchen to check on the entrées. I'd been on the job for less than a month, and I already knew to be relieved when the job included the use of kitchen facilities on-site. Granted, the word *kitchen* appeared to mean different things in different places, but anything beat having to prep everything back at the restaurant in the early morning, before the regular kitchen staff arrived.

Or worse yet, having to work around them and risk the wrath of Chef Stephan.

Cheryl, my best line chef—a short, thin woman with wild red curls—smiled as I entered the spacious kitchen in the building basement. "Hey, boss, ready for the soup yet?"

I glanced at the soup bowls lined up along the stainless steel counter like overturned porcelain hats. "Not yet. I'll page you when the first salad plate empties. We should be able to get all four carts in the service elevator, but if you need to take a second trip—"

"We'll be fine. Relax. We've done this before."

"Sorry." Corporate events made me jumpy. It was too strange to be on the other side of the serving table.

"Everything's going smoothly." She made a shooing gesture, sweeping me out of the kitchen. "Don't worry about us."

As I took the service elevator back to the top floor, I wondered why Cheryl didn't have my job. She had more experience, knew the city and the clients. Did the company have a policy of not hiring from within? I needed to get around to reading the employee handbook.

As the elevator door opened I saw Kenny and another waiter standing by the door, each carrying a large tray of dirty glassware.

"I don't even know if he's—" Kenny broke off as the door opened. His eyes widened when he saw me. He blushed. Kitchens can be capricious places. Maybe the last catering chef had discouraged talk among the waiters. I gave them both a nod and a smile and held the door open to show that it was fine with me. As long as the guests didn't hear, what did I care what they talked about? Kenny was a good waiter. I made a mental note to have him on crew as often as possible.

* * *

"The swishy writer?" Chef Stephan scowled at me over the soup stock he was tasting.

I winced. Kenny didn't miss much, did he? "He's one of the best I've worked with, efficient and courteous. The customers like him."

Chef shrugged. "To each his own. He gives me the creeps, but if you want him on your team permanently, I don't care. It's your stomach."

I gritted my teeth. "Thank you, Chef."

At least he was letting me have a say in my crew.

I went back to my desk to get ready for my consultation with Skeletor's mom, wondering if her daughter's kitchen was big enough. Preparing our signature heavy hors d'oeuvres would be more pleasant and practical away from Chef Stephan's toxic kitchen.

Look for Bread, Salt and Wine
from Love is a Light
Spring 2015